*She could not breathe.*

❧❧

He stopped walking and stood shirtless, his chest slathered with blood and war paint. His breechcloth rode low on his hips; leggings were tied around his sinewy thighs and at his knees. He had long legs and long arms, and in his right hand he held a knife.

There was blood on the blade.

She scrabbled away from him; he hurried toward her, transferring his knife to his left hand and showing her his empty right palm. She shook her head wordlessly.

He said to her, "*Mahwah.*"

It was the voice.

Soft in her ear, the voice she had heard whispering through the forest.

She cleared her throat, but no sound came out. She tried again to move away from him, slipping in the mud.

He glided easily to her side and grabbed her wrist. He smelled of smoke. He braced himself and pulled her up, grinning faintly as she tried to ensure that her body was shielded from his gaze while at the same time keeping her balance.

Then all thought of herself fled as she caught sight of the scene behind him.

❧❧

*"Once Upon a Time . . ." is timely again in
these retold fairy tales:*

# THE STORYTELLER'S DAUGHTER
*by Cameron Dokey*

# BEAUTY SLEEP
*by Cameron Dokey*

# SNOW
*by Tracy Lynn*

# MIDNIGHT PEARLS
*by Debbie Viguié*

# SCARLET MOON
*by Debbie Viguié*

# SUNLIGHT and SHADOW
*by Cameron Dokey*

# SPIRITED
*by Nancy Holder*

*From Simon Pulse
Published by Simon & Schuster*

# SPIRITED

Nancy Holder

SIMON PULSE
New York   London   Toronto   Sydney

This book is a work of fiction. Any references to historical events, real people, or real locales are used fictitiously. Other names, characters, places, and incidents are the product of the author's imagination, and any resemblance to actual events or locales or persons, living or dead, is entirely coincidental.

SIMON PULSE
An imprint of Simon & Schuster Children's Publishing Division
1230 Avenue of the Americas, New York, NY 10020

SIMON PULSE and colophon are registered trademarks of Simon & Schuster, Inc.

Designed by Debra Sfetsios
The text of this book was set in Adobe Jenson.

Printed in the United States of America
First Simon Pulse edition November 2004
2 4 6 8 10 9 7 5 3 1

Library of Congress Control Number 2004107972
ISBN 0-689-87063-9

✦✦✦✦✦✦

To my beautiful and wonderful daughter,
Belle Claire Christine Holder, who is a shining spirit.

Nia ktachwahnen, Wauntheet Monnitoow.

It takes a village to write a book.
Wneeweh: my editors, past and present: Amanda Berger,
Bethany Buck, and Lisa Clancy, who shares my love of the
1992 version of the film The Last of the Mohicans and was the
one to say yes. My agent, Howard Morhaim and his
assistant Erin McGhee. Rebecca Morhaim, Aquai. To
my friends, family, and Kearny Villa Road homies. To my
JoysofResearch helpers and the women of SF-FW's.
To Liz Cratty, Kym Toia, and Christy Holt.
To Daniel Day-Lewis.

✦✦✦✦✦✦

*As I walk, as I walk*
*The universe is walking with me*
*In beauty it walks before me*
*In beauty it walks behind me*
*In beauty it walks below me*
*In beauty it walks above me*
*Beauty is on every side*
*As I walk, I walk with Beauty.*

**Traditional Navajo Prayer**

*This is a medicine story.*
*It tells of a Way.*
*The Way is called "achwahndowagan"*
*in the language of the People.*
*The Way is called "love" in the language of Mahwah.*
*The Way is called "Mahwah" in the language of my spirit.*
*It is my Way.*

**—Wusamequin, Medicine Man of the People of
the River, in the Land Beyond**

# ❖ Chapter One ❖

The forest was magical, a world Isabella Stevens could never have imagined, a land undreamed of. If anyone had ever told her that such a place existed, she would have called him a liar or a lunatic, despite the fact that such harsh words ought never to pass the lips of a well-bred lady.

Isabella had been carefully brought up. She was the daughter of Surgeon Phillip Stevens, who was an officer and a gentleman in King George's Royal Army, and she had been trained since infancy to always remember that her behavior reflected directly on him. She had learned her lessons; she was sixteen now, a young woman, and a credit, so she was told, to her family name.

Since the death of her beloved mother, Emily Elizabeth Stevens, Isabella Anne was the only lady to grace Dr. Stevens's household. Sometimes it seemed a heavy responsibility to take charge of Mama's duties; but today, in the forest, she was glad her father needed her help at his new posting at Fort William Henry. The wildness of the forest excited her. As she looked this way and that, her cheeks warmed with pleasure. Another chestnut curl escaped the circlet braided atop her head, moist with the May warmth. She tucked it behind her ear, grazing her golden, rose-shaped earbob, and continued to drink in the beauty surrounding her.

With one gray doeskin glove to her broad-brimmed straw hat, she ducked beneath an overhanging branch of brilliant autumn foliage. The colors astonished her. The dead leaves jittered free of the branch, and she raised her face in delight as they showered her with color. Gold and scarlet gleamed like the coats of the four-and-twenty soldiers of the 35th Regiment of Foot, who were escorting her and her father to Fort William Henry. Deep, rich purple glowed like the heather on the misty moors back home in England. Silver sparkled like the silver locket she wore on a black velvet band around her neck. Inside the oval of silver rested two tiny portraits—a miniature of Papa on the left; and on the right, Mama, dead and buried these nine long months.

Entranced, she pressed her other soft leather glove against the cream edging of her pale green, wool traveling cloak. Mrs. Cora DeWitt, a neighbor who had been extraordinarily kind to Isabella and her father back in Albany, had advised her to lace her corset tight, to spare her back as she rode the long hours sidesaddle on her little roan mare, Dulcie. Isabella had done as Mrs. DeWitt suggested, but she was beginning to suspect that she might have overdone it. Her breathing was constricted and she was a trifle dizzy.

She wasn't certain what to do about it, and unclear if it would be proper to ask her father to help her loosen her stays. But neither was she certain she would be able to manage it on her own.

Three sat on horseback as the company journeyed through the forest. Riding very closely beside her on a bay Galloway gelding was her father. He and Isabella had lived one year in the Colonies.

The third rider was Major Whyte, who had been in the Americas for three years. He was in charge of their escort, and he sat very tall upon his cavalry saddle and thick saddle blanket beneath. His Friesian was pitch black and he guided it expertly with a double bridle. His spine straight as a ramrod, his head high beneath his tricorne hat, he was the perfect British officer.

Samuel was his Christian name, and she blushed at the occasional glances he directed her way. He was a broad-shouldered man and pleasing to look at, for all that he could have been her brother, with his oval face and queue of natural, deep brown hair. In other features they departed: His eyes were hazel; hers were a very heavily lashed deep blue. Her mother used to tell her that her eyes were her best feature.

"The same cannot be said of your hair, alas," Mama would go on to say. She would speak of "taming" the masses of thick, unruly curls that tumbled over her daughter's shoulders and down to the small of her back. She would often chide Isabella for her

hair's "wildness," as if it were Isabella's fault that it was
so hard to care for, and that she herself should do
something about it. Even now, as they rode, yet
another tendril escaped from the braided circlet she
had arranged atop her head. It bobbed against her
cheek with a faint tickle like the kiss of a butterfly.
She supposed she looked rather strange, glassy-eyed
from lack of air, and her hair springing loose in mad
ringlets, like Chinese fireworks.

So . . . perhaps it was not admiration that caused
Major Whyte to look at her so often. Perhaps he was
simply fascinated by her bizarre appearance. Or perhaps he was wishing her away. He had strenuously
objected to her traveling with her father to Fort
William Henry. He had said it was far too dangerous
for a lady, with savages in the wilderness and pestilence
in the garrison, and that she should stay in Albany.

Though her father agreed with the major, Isabella
would not hear of it.

*So far we have been safe. Perhaps our luck will hold,* she
thought. *And as for the pestilence, Papa is bringing the soldiers the medicine that will cure it. I've naught to fear on
that score.*

A sudden movement caught her attention. Her
eyes widened in wonder as a bright red cardinal fluttered from inside a hollow in a thick tree trunk. It
cocked its head at her like a toy cuckoo in a clock. It
chirped at her once; then rose effortlessly into the
canopy of gold and scarlet, disappearing into the
azure sky.

The wilderness was a busy, noisy place. Birdsong trilled as squirrels chittered up and down the branches of the birch, maple, chestnut, and pine trees. The leaves blazed in their glory. The soldiers marched, their leather boots thudding on the forest path. In a quick intake of air, she breathed in her horse's clean scent and the odor of the damp, black earth.

*To think that I almost missed this . . . that I almost consented when Mama and Papa begged me to remain in England, safe and securely buried in the country with Aunt Mary-Elizabeth. It was the first time I refused either of them anything.*

*Something told my heart to come here, to this strange New World. I just knew that I had to leave London and journey across the water. It was as if an angel whispered in my ear that I was wanted here.*

*And good thing, too, now that Mama is gone. Though my father claims that his work fills the emptiness she left behind, he would not have lasted a fortnight in the Americas without me.*

She fingered the locket around her neck, a lump forming in her throat.

*The second time I disobeyed Papa was coming with him now, on this journey. When Major Whyte explained how dangerous it was, he begged me to stay in town. But as before, something told me to come with him. And as before, I listened.*

*I wonder what will come of that decision.*

At that moment, lacy yellow-green ferns shifted and bobbed as something moved among them. She caught her breath—or tried to. Then a delicate deer raised its head from the ferns. It was exquisite, its head so thin and its innocent brown eyes soft and gentle. It did not move a muscle, but gazed placidly at the young Englishwoman riding through its home.

Isabella leaned over and tapped her father's arm. He was riding closely beside her, keeping a protective watch over her. When she had his attention, she gestured with her head toward the deer. Dr. Stevens followed her line of vision and cocked his salt-and-pepper head beneath his three-cornered hat. His smile was a joy to her. He didn't smile so often these days.

"Papa, it's so beautiful, is it not?" she murmured.

Her father nodded without speaking. He reached over and took her hand, giving it a squeeze.

Eagerly she added, "The wilderness is so much more wonderful than I had expec—"

"Miss Stevens, I beg of you, keep silent," Major Whyte said quietly from his position just ahead of them. He turned in his saddle as he spoke. The gold buttons of his coat flashed in the sun as he touched his gloved hand to his lips. He was being stern, and yet there was courtesy there, and respect.

Cheeks burning, she inclined her head in a gesture of apology. He gave her a small nod, his look lingering on her face. Blushing harder, she lowered her gaze to her gloves.

*He stares at me because I look strange,* she insisted to herself.

When she glanced back at the deer, it had vanished from sight.

They rode on, bridles jingling, the black leather boots of the soldiers thudding against the dirt. The men wore the peaked mitre caps of their regiment and were quite smartly turned out in their uniforms and knapsacks, all matching like lead nursery toys. The sight of them filled her with pride. With men like these in her regiments, England would prevail once again over her enemies.

*Let it be soon,* she prayed. *Too much blood has been spilled in these colonies; there has been too much death for a land so young and fair.*

She soaked in the vista surrounding her, taking in the lacy ferns, the shadowed woods, the dappled bower of colorful leaves. It was difficult to believe that this wonderland harbored death, but it did, and they must move through it as quickly as possible to the fort. The British were at war—with France, again—and the Indians who dwelled in these dense woodlands had taken up sides. Some fought for France, and some had allied themselves with Isabella's sovereign, King George II of England.

But none of them was to be trusted any more than one would trust a wild animal. She shuddered at the memory of the Indians she had seen in Albany— half-naked, copper-colored men adorned with bizarre tattoos all over their bodies, some even extending across their faces. With their flintlocks and tomahawks strapped across their backs, they swaggered through the streets as if they owned them. They wore their contempt as they wore their battle scars, displayed for all to see. Feathers and beads decorated tufts of black hair on the tops of their heads, arranged in a fashion to give their enemies something to grab onto while scalping them.

She tried to keep herself from forming an image of a scalped man.

She had not been able to understand how civilized men could have anything to do with such savages. Her father had explained to her that the natives hadn't the same sorts of minds as civilized people. But all the same, they had the ability to fight. The French were using them very poorly, promising them all sorts of outlandish things in order to secure their help in their war against the British: Gold, jewels, rum, gin, and brandy. Huge quantities of drink. Firewater, as they called it. Not a man among them could handle it. And what need had savages for fine jewels and gold bracelets? They had no sense of taste or refinement. It had to be the sparkle that attracted them.

The British watched these exchanges . . . and learned. They bartered more reasonable items: beads that the Indians used for their clothing and also as money; blankets and axes, that sort of thing. Seeing that the Indians could not be expected to sort out complicated loyalties, the English simplified their agreements with the local chiefs. The King was spoken of as their Great White Father, and the British authorities were his representatives. The Indians were called the children of the Great White Father, and it was quite appropriate. They were simple, like children—at times surly and stubborn; at others, impulsive and quite unable to restrain themselves when the urge to violence came upon them.

And that urge came swift and sure, as the hapless settlers in these parts could attest: the Hurons, allies of the French, had torn through settlements not far from here, butchering and scalping the men and capturing the women and children, either to torture to death or keep as slaves.

As if he could read her darkening thoughts, her father checked the pistol tucked into his belt. His powder horn was looped around a clip on his saddle. He was not a warlike man; he was a physician, and they were riding to the fort on a mission of mercy. But he was also an officer, and he had seen battle before. He could be counted on if there was trouble.

Still, Isabella couldn't believe that he would need to use his firearm. Because their traveling party carried medicines to Fort William Henry, they were noncombatants, by the rules of war. Instead of a drummer, their company was led by a soldier carrying a white flag, the universal symbol of peace. Surely even primitives would honor their banner and grant them safe passage.

She glanced anxiously at her father, studying his profile. She saw new lines in his forehead and creases around his mouth. This year in the Colonies had aged him.

And it had killed her mother, who now slept beneath a weeping angel in the churchyard in Albany. Her personal physician had declared her death to be a result of nervous exhaustion. From the moment they had debarked their brig, the *Necessity*, she had hated this land and begged to go home. Though disappointed to be parted from his wife and child, Papa made all the arrangements to send them back. Aunt Mary-Elizabeth's it was to be, after all.

But then war had been declared between Britain and France the following May, both at home and in their American possessions. Sea travel was out of the question.

"We are trapped!" her mother had shrieked, grabbing onto Isabella as if she were drowning. Her blue eyes nearly spun, she was so overwrought. She clung to her child and shouted at her husband, "My child and I will die in this godforsaken wilderness!"

And so Mama had.

As Isabella rode motherless beside her father now, she felt a sharp pang, then resolutely forced it away. She grieved only at night, and only alone, when the shadows cloaked her from her father. She would not for the world disturb him with her tears. Their nation was at war, and his skills must be at the ready for the wounded and the sick. Mourning was a luxury denied him. It must therefore be denied to his daughter as well.

*Later, we will weep for Mama. But not now.*
*We have men to save.*

# ❖ Chapter Two ❖

On the craggy cliff overlooking waves of purple-ridged mountaintops, Wusamequin, the young medicine man of the People of the River, raged and mourned his dead.

Surrounded by maples, chestnut trees, and arrow-straight pines, he sat cross-legged as he leaned forward toward the campfire he had built of rocks and birch wood. With his jaw set and hard, he wafted the holy, fragrant smoke over his face and head. His dark, deep-set eyes watered. He had unbound his black hair, and it hung past his shoulders and over his chest, where twin tattoos of bears crouched on the bulge of his pectorals.

He was in deep mourning. A thick black line crossed his chest, etched with smaller tattoos of triangles with their points hanging downward, to symbolize tears. Fresh tattoos of triangles ran up and down his biceps and encircled his wrists. With each moon that passed with no honor to his name, he had sought out the pain of the tattooing in order to feel alive. His body cried out in despair. His heart pounded the drum of grief.

But Wusamequin was a very private man, and he did not weep.

Though the air was chilly, he wore only his loincloth, leggings, and moccasins. He felt nothing, and everything. Mindful of his shame, he had visited the sweat lodge alone. He had chanted and prayed, but he had found no relief from the fury that boiled inside him.

Then he doused himself in the icy lake to slake off the poisons that he had sweated from his body and his spirit. Purified, he was now prepared to seek counsel from the land of the spirits as he marked the anniversary of the murder of his family.

He chanted for a time, low and steadily, his voice like teardrops on the body of the Great Mother, from whom the world had formed. Time passed, and his voice grew still. Feeling more centered inside his sorrow, he pushed with the sides of his feet and rose to a standing position. He was tall for a man of his people; his name was a good name, speaking of strength. It had also been the name of a number of illustrious chiefs of his people.

He reached into his medicine pouch and sprinkled the ashes with dried tobacco, bee balm, snakewort, and tobacco. The mixture disappeared inside the mouths of orange and red. He rubbed some of it onto his face and his arms, then covered his eyes with his fingertips, forcing back a heavy sob.

He lowered his arms to his sides, took a deep breath, and raised his chin. He was Wusamequin, and he had the right to speak to the spirits.

"Thirteen moons have passed since my wife and

child were stolen from me," he told the east wind. "From the chill snowy moon, which is Wolf Moon, to the thaw of Pink Moon; from hot Sturgeon Moon to bountiful Harvest Moon; to the darkest moon, which is Cold Moon, I have mourned my dead for an entire cycle of the Mother's life."

The wind answered back, whistling through the branches of the trees in a single voice, like the flute of a brave who has lost his chance at love.

*Your time will come.*

He turned to the west wind and spread wide his arms. "Thirteen moons since I swore I would paint my tomahawk with the blood of their killers."

*Your time will come.*

He pulled his tomahawk from the leather strap on his breechcloth and showed the spirits of the north his unblemished blade. He shook it at the sunny sky.

"Thirteen moons, and my scalp pole stands empty!"

*Your time will come.*

To the south, he cried, "Why do you not send British soldiers to me, so my wife and my infant son can walk the Road of Stars? I am dishonored, and my loved ones go unavenged!"

He threw back his head and cried out in frustration as he spoke to the firmament. His voice echoed like a rifle shot through the valleys of the purple mountains. *Unavenged . . . unavenged . . .* it was a bitter chant of rage and despair.

"I cannot fail in this!" he shouted to the earth below. "My spirit is worthless until I fulfill my vow!"

As if in answer, an icy wind whipped low across the forest floor, raising a whirlpool of desiccated pine needles and leaves the color of blood. The wind grew stronger; its force slapped his hair against his hollow cheeks like a stinging lash. He did not feel it. His chest was heaving. He was dizzy with fury.

The wind carried the leaves and needles into the fire, feeding it; the flames rose higher, feeding the heat in his heart, the heat of his anger. If only he had a Yangee soldier within his grasp; he would make the white devil pay for the destruction of his life.

He would make the Yangee pay for days.

For the death of his young wife, and of his tiny son, only days old . . .

By every drop of blood inside his body, by every tear he had not shed, he would make him pay.

He threw back his head and whispered to the spirits, "Give me my vengeance. I am dying day by day."

*Your time will come.*

"I am tired of waiting! I am a man! I do not sit by the fire like an old squaw!"

The sky darkened; the wood crackled and snapped, and Wusamequin began to dance. He moved his lean body around the campfire, fists clenched, biceps flexed; he danced of torture and revenge.

The spirits of the air watched, and they approved.

The dance of a medicine man conjured powerful magic; and Miantonomi, the father of Wusamequin, had been a shaman unrivaled in power among his people. But his father had died from one of the many horrible diseases the white skins brought with them from their villages across the great water. His skin erupted in sores; his body shook; he vomited black blood. And there had been nothing his son could do to save him. There was no magic in his medicine bag more powerful than the white skins' disease.

As soon as his father breathed the last breath, Wusamequin had been elected to his office by the elder women of the tribe, as was their right. They had brought him a beaded belt and led him to a fresh wigwam, where all his possessions had been lovingly arranged for him. His father's things were burned in his old wigwam that very night, to prevent the sickness that had permeated them from harming Wusamequin.

He had not felt ready to devote himself to his tribe's spiritual welfare, but he had accepted the honor. His wife had glowed with pride. And she had loved him well his first night as shaman. Their son had grown in her belly after that.

Wusamequin had worked hard to learn what his father had not had time to teach him. He felt strong medicine within him, but he had not yet learned how to call it forth.

Then his wife and child were killed. In less than two years, he had lost his father, his woman, and his seed. It was more than he could bear; he withdrew, and no enticement could bring him back into the heart of the community. Not even the beautiful maiden Odina, who had loved him before he married his wife, and who loved him still.

It was obvious to everyone in the village that his spirit was slowly dying. His grief and hatred were consuming him like wolves starving in winter.

The loss of another medicine man so soon after the death of the great Miantonomi would be a blow to his people. They were already severely weakened by the wars and the constant encroachment of the pale newcomers. The white skin settlers fished out the rivers and cleared the forest to plant their corn; the forest animals were therefore easier to hunt, and the newcomers killed them all.

The white skins brought death in many forms, and the apple-cheeked children of the People of the River lost their fat and became gaunt like old men. Their mothers spent endless hours foraging for groundnuts, leeks, and wild onions. Their vast supplies of cherries, black currants, and blue figs shrank. On the shore of the great waters, their prized oyster beds had been picked clean. The rivers of herring, shad, and trout had thinned out.

As the People grew hungry, the hunters ranged farther away in search of game. The warriors went with them, so desperate were the People for food. And that was when the white devils had struck: when the young men were gone, and Wusamequin and the elders had been left to care for the women and children.

In that, too, he had failed his people.

But the villagers still looked to their warriors and to Wusamequin to save them. Wusamequin concentrated on learning his shaman's Way: he alone could part the veil of smokes between the world of men and the world of ghosts and spirits. He was a spirit warrior who walked in moccasins no other man dared to wear.

But he did not wear them comfortably. He did not feel like a spirit warrior. No feathers graced his hair. No woman shared his bed.

And so he danced, red-eyed and tearless, and remembered a time when his wife—whose name he did not speak—had whispered to him, "My great husband, I am so happy in this moment that if I died in the next, I would only laugh."

She had not laughed. She had died screaming for her baby as two British soldiers shot her with their muskets and left her bleeding and broken. She had died in agony. And her baby . . .

His baby . . .

"Bring me peace. Bring me relief," Wusamequin sang as he danced. In his pain, he ran his tomahawk across his palm, hissing from the cruel kiss of his blade. It was painted red now, but his blood would not feed its hunger. His tomahawk was starving.

His heart was starving.

"Give me peace!" he shouted.

Another wind shot through the clearing. Sparks flared into the sky, sizzling against his bare chest and shoulders.

"Give me back my loved ones!"

He stomped his feet; he whirled in a circle. The drums of the spirits cannonaded through the treetops; clouds gathered above him and crouched, low and ready.

A third time the wind gathered its forces, and this time the spirit of the wind blew his essence into Wusamequin's mourning fire.

The smoke billowed and coiled like the whitewater of a rapids; then it thickened and rose in a column, a waterfall of smoke rising up into the air. Wusamequin danced, passing his tomahawk through the scented mists, through the veils that were parting between this world and the other.

The smoke undulated as it found form, and Wusamequin fell to his knees in exhaustion. He rose up, kneeling with his arms crossed over his chest.

The column roared and Wusamequin whispered, *"Aquai."* Hello.

It rushed and billowed, and then his spirit guide stepped into the world.

His guide's name was Great Bear, and he loomed at least six hands higher than his human nephew, Wusamequin. He was covered in brownish black fur, a giant of the forest. Great Bear had come to Wusamequin six winters earlier, during the youth's initiation into the world of men, first appearing when Wusamequin had left the tribe to walk his vision quest. Miantonomi had been pleased by his son's adoption by Great Bear, who was a powerful totem.

"We have need of such an ally in these hard times," Miantonomi had told the proud, happy youth. "This speaks well of your favor with the ancestors, my son."

Now Great Bear held out his powerful, sharp paws in greeting, each as wide as Wusamequin's chest, and bellowed at the man who, in his despair, had summoned him. Great Bear's head was as big as the campfire, and each of his eyes was larger than Wusamequin's fist. His teeth were sharp and very white, and he smelled of the other place where he dwelled—of sweet grass and clear waters, and air that had never been breathed by men.

Of the Land Beyond, the paradise where the People lived after they left the world, in preparation for the journey on the Road of Stars.

*Wusamequin, my nephew,* Great Bear said. *You are suffering. I am glad you have called me.*

Wusamequin decided to dance his conversation with Great Bear. He had voiced his rage, and so he would remain silent out of respect for the Great One. Though he had shouted his demands to the spirits, it had been his dance that had called Great Bear from the invisible world to him.

Wusamequin rose and spread forth his arms. *The spirits say my time will come. I am tired of waiting for justice, my uncle.*

*I understand, my nephew. Turn around.*

His heart filling with hope, Wusamequin obeyed, exposing his back to the enormous bear.

Great Bear extended his paw and traced the scar that ran the length of Wusamequin's spine, beginning at the base of his skull and trailing to the small of his back. The wound had cut very deep.

The British soldiers had assumed that it had killed him. Knowing that the braves had left to hunt, they attacked without warning, without provocation. He had been in the sweat lodge when he heard his wife screaming. He had burst out of the lodge and run to the wigwam, run as hard as he could. . . .

*Clear your mind, my nephew,* Great Bear urged him. *Your fury blinds you. It fragments you.*

As he turned back around, Wusamequin stared unsmiling at his beloved spirit guide. Both his father and his guide had taught Wusamequin that this life was both a journey and a test. As a man and a warrior, Wusamequin must prove his valor and his courage; he must die with a clean conscience that he had done his best at all times. He must provide results in order to be able to face seven generations of his ancestors. He must have triumphs to share when it came time for him to count coup—to speak of his victories over the challenges laid before him. He must prove to them that he was worthy to sit with them at the council fires, or he would be banished from their company and wander in shame and degradation for all time.

The blood trickled from Wusamequin's palm into the fire, each droplet hissing as it hit the flames. It must not be his blood only that nourished the fires of this world.

His enemies must burn for what they had done.

*You are my guide, Great Bear,* he reminded the huge creature. *It is your duty to accompany me on my path, and to assist me so that I may count coup.*

Great Bear growled and waved his paws. His jaws opened, closed. Saliva roped from his great teeth. Then he lowered his head and raised it again, nodding at the shaman.

*And so I shall, my human nephew. I promise you this very day, I will show you the path you must take to answer the true prayers of your heart.*

Wusamequin's heart soared. Hope fed his fierce anger.

*You will help me hunt soldiers to kill?* he persisted. *Yangee warriors to feed my tomahawk? Scalps to proclaim the restoration of my honor, so that my dead son may also sit proudly at the council fire of my ancestors? That he may count coup on his own behalf, and then walk the Road of Stars with his mother?*

His spirit guide growled at him again and lowered his paws. Then he spoke in the language of this world's bears.

*Proud, angry man, I will give you what I say I will.*

Still balanced on his hind legs, the bear ambled in a slow circle and tumbled forward onto his front paws. Then he lumbered into the forest, looking over his shoulder once, as if to urge his disciple to follow.

Wusamequin trotted behind Great Bear into the thick stands of trees. Above his head, the storm clouds gathered and began to rumble. They covered the sun, and as Wusamequin entered the forest, he was cloaked in darkness. But he knew the way among the trees and streams as surely as his son had known the way to his mother's breast.

Without hesitation, the young medicine man followed Great Bear deep into the woods.

# ❧ Chapter Three ❧

*D*id I hear something?

It could have been a man's shout echoing off a mountain. Or the cry of an eagle, or the roar of a wild animal.

Or it could have been the crashing of the breathtaking waterfall they were approaching. From perhaps fifty feet above the treetops, the falls cascaded into a wide stream that meandered beside their path.

Still, Isabella's attention had been caught; her senses were on alert. She glanced around to see if anyone else had heard anything unusual. Judging by her father's steady expression, he had not. Major Whyte, too, continued to ride ahead, and gave no sign that he found anything amiss.

She settled back in her saddle, wishing again that she could find a way to loosen her corset. She found herself envying the Indian women, who did not wear them. Of course, their men treated them like slaves. Or chattel—they even traded them for horses.

*I would sooner die than live like an Indian squaw.*

There it was again.

"Isabella . . ."

*It is my name!*

23

Lips parting, she narrowed her eyes and cocked her head. The sound had been very soft, a whisper on the wind, maybe even a memory stirring in her mind.

It came again: "Isabella . . ."

She gasped. A glance at her unconcerned father told her that, clearly, he had not heard it.

*Is my mind too starved for air? Am I hearing things?*

She pressed against her chest and bowed slightly inward to give her lungs a chance to expand. The lace of her collar tickled her under the chin; otherwise, her efforts bore no results. Her father raised a brow and she dropped her hand away in mild frustration.

"Isabella," came the whisper again. Only it wasn't *Isabella* precisely. It was something close, something similar . . .

"Mahwah . . ."

"Yes?" she whispered very softly, in a tone so low she herself didn't hear it.

As soon as the word came out of her mouth, a sudden darkness blotted the sky.

"What the devil?" her father blurted as he pulled his horse up short.

A murmur rose among the men. The sky grew darker still, covering the 35th like a black net. Gray sank from the sky toward the earth. The colors drained away from the leaves and the bright British uniforms. Her gloves were a dull, flat color, as if she had plunged them into a muddy river.

"A storm is coming," Dr. Stevens said quickly to her. "That's all, my dear."

Isabella's mount chuffed anxiously. A chill rushed up her spine and she gathered the reins as she would pull a blanket up to her chin in her bed when she was cold or uneasy.

All her life, she had had a terrible fear of storms.

Coming abreast of her and her father, Major Whyte frowned up at the shadowed sky and said to Dr. Stevens, "It's going to rain, sir. I suggest we seek shelter. I can have the men pitch tents."

"Is that safe?" Isabella asked, aware that by questioning him in front of his men, she was being quite rude. "I . . . that is, you had suggested we must be quickly through these woods."

"I did," he retorted, knitting his brows, clearly vexed. "I am thinking of your comfort, Miss Stevens." He gestured to his troops. "If we were all men here, I would insist we ride through the storm. But you are a young lady, and I must take that into account. And as you are not a stranger to these Colonies, you may know that the weather can be quite severe."

"I can manage quite well," she assured him, unwilling to be an inconvenience.

But a terrible sense of foreboding gripped her that went beyond her childish fear. The more she considered it, the more certain she was that something had called her name. And now something very bad was about to happen. She could sense it in every part of her being.

"Forgive me, sir." Her gaze matched his in steadiness. "I do not mean to dispute your decision. But

I . . . something is *wrong*. I thought I heard a . . . voice. Did you not?"

"A voice?" he echoed, and she nodded.

"Very quiet. Like a . . . whisper." She was at a loss how to explain it to him.

"No, miss, I did not," he replied. "But that may only mean that my hearing is less well-turned than yours," he added politely.

"I heard no voice," her father added, his tone low and uneasy. "What did it say, Isabella?"

"I thought . . . I thought I heard my own name, Papa," she answered.

His eyes narrowed, and she wondered if he was recalling the night her mother died. There had been a storm that night, too. The wind howled like an Irish banshee, promising death. Tree branches flogged the green wood shutters; thunder shook the rafters.

In a panic Isabella had suddenly leaped out of bed and rushed barefoot to her mother's rooms. She had been the one to discover the cold body of Emily Stevens.

After the funeral, her father had asked, "How did you know to go to her?"

"Indeed, I did not know," she had replied, weeping, a glass of sherry between her ice-cold palms. "Else I should have been there in time to save her."

Eventually her father dropped the matter. She had no explanation for it, and it sat between them now and then, of a night when they were both lonely, she supposed.

"Where did the sound come from?" Major Whyte asked her now, in the forest. A wind was rising, and with it, her anxiety.

She flushed. "I—I'm not certain. I'm sorry—"

"Sir, we must be prepared," Major Whyte said to Dr. Stevens.

"Agreed," her father murmured.

Moving as one, the two British officers drew their pistols. They would have one shot each. Isabella wished she had a pistol; but then, she had no idea how to use one.

*These men are here for my protection*, she reminded herself as the phalanx of soldiers shifted about in the gloom. She could feel the tension growing among the ranks. *They are trained for it.*

Shadows crawled down the trees and spread across the earth. It was nearly as dark as night.

Major Whyte said to the men, "Look alive. Alert me if you see any movement in the brush."

"And 'ow we going to do that, when it's black as tar?" one of the soldiers muttered beneath his breath. Though she could barely see it now she knew his hair was an impossible scarlet, and there were freckles across his nose. "It's not natural, this. There's a hex on this place. We ought to run for our lives."

"Silence, Ben Schoten," Major Whyte said with deadly stillness. "I give the orders here."

The soldier shifted his weight. "Sir, this be witch-craft." He glanced in Isabella's direction. "Meaning no disrespect, sir, but we've a female with us, and—"

"That is enough!" The major raised his voice. "One more word and I'll have you flogged here and now, instead of later!"

Major Whyte leaned forward in his saddle like a wolf about to leap onto its prey. Schoten flinched as if he had been struck. Officers held tremendous power over their subordinates, and Major Whyte could be merciless if he chose to. Isabella knew discipline was strict in the Army, and Schoten had certainly been trained not to question his superiors.

But Schoten was right. Something was clearly amiss. In less than a minute, the forest had been plunged into impenetrable gloom. At this rate, they wouldn't be able to see their own hands in the time it took to speak of it.

Whyte's horse whinnied anxiously and stamped his forelegs. He reined him in and patted his neck, far more sympathetic to his unease than he had been to Ben Schoten's.

"Dr. Stevens, please, sir," he said, "I want you to take Miss Stevens and—"

A huge shape crashed from the nearest thicket of pine and chestnut trees, followed by a loud bellow. The roar ripped through the forest; several of the soldiers shouted in terror. Isabella tried to follow the attacker with her gaze. It was enormous.

It was happening so fast. As she blinked, the

shadow fell upon the men; one of them shrieked as it charged him, swiping at him, knocking him down and trampling him.

Isabella screamed.

"Indians!" someone shouted.

"It's a bear!" Ben Schoten screamed.

"Present arms! Fire at will!" Major Whyte commanded his men as he took aim. His horse reared just as his firearm discharged. The shape let out another roar and lurched into the mass of soldiers, who were scattering as it advanced.

"Damme," Major Whyte gritted his teeth.

Then Dr. Stevens shot his pistol. He missed as well.

"Dr. Stevens, sir, follow me!" the major bellowed.

Major Whyte reached across Isabella and grabbed her reins from her hands. He put his heels to his own horse and galloped with her off the path, herding her horse toward the waterfall, in the opposite direction of their attacker. In the descending darkness, the white crests of crashing water at the base of the falls glowed a strange white. Droplets pelted her face and hair. She realized she had dropped her hat; she realized, also, that she was on the verge of fainting.

Isabella tried to look over her shoulder, but the lace of her collar obscured her view. She tried to catch her breath and could not; her heart was pounding feverishly, and the world was growing dim.

Her father drew up beside her and Major Whyte.

The major handed her reins to him and wheeled back around, returning to the wild scene behind them.

Men were screaming. Flintlocks erupted, sending a ricochet of percussion through the chestnuts and birches. The shape growled.

There was more screaming among the troops. Isabella's horse threw back its head, whinnying hysterically. Muskets flared in the dying light. The crack of their shots echoed in Isabella's bones.

"Oh, my God," her father said. He grabbed her shoulder. "Don't look."

"What is happening?" she cried, half-turning in her saddle. The dark world spun. "Papa," she began. "I can't breathe. . . ."

"Don't look," he ordered her again. Then he grabbed her and pulled her against his chest. "Don't, poppet," he said, which was a name he used to call her when she was little.

She tilted back her head and studied his face, which was rapidly disappearing as the forest grew darker. His jaw was clenched; his mouth was pursed and grim.

Behind them, more shrieking pierced her ears. More firing. The bear roared like a demon.

*Ben Schoten was right,* she thought. *We should have run away.*

From his position about thirty lengths from the waterfall, Wusamequin's heart soared as he witnessed the carnage unfolding in the dark forest below.

*British soldiers!* Though it was difficult to see, there was no mistaking the red uniforms of the Yangees. His spirit guide had led him to them, and darkened their vision so that he could destroy as many of them as possible. With ferocity and courage, Great Bear fought among them, keeping them busy and thinning their numbers to give Wusamequin time to gather his warriors. As Wusamequin watched, Great Bear felled two of the Yangees with a powerful sweep of his arm, slamming them to the ground as if they were fat trout.

Uttering a single war cry, Wusamequin turned around and raced back the way he had come. His chest rose and fell; sweat beaded his forehead. His legs pumped. Like any good adult male, he could run all day if he had to; it was nothing to cover the distance between the forest path and the village.

He only prayed he could do so fast enough for the braves to kill all the English before any got away. He had seen only one man on horseback, while the others marched on foot. He couldn't make the assumption, however, that he had seen the entire party.

"Thank you, Great Bear," he whispered.

Today, on the exact day his family had been killed thirteen moons before, he would finally have his vengeance.

He screamed his war cry as he ran, calling the braves to arms. By the time he reached the first wigwam, the braves had begun to assemble. The war chief, Sasious, was there, pulling his leather shirt over his breechcloth and leggings. His coup feathers fluttered in the wind. Wusamequin's friend chubby Keshkecho was there, his tomahawk in his right fist.

Their tribal leader, the great Sachem Oneko, strode toward Wusamequin as the medicine man raced to the center of the cluster of men. Heavily muscled, the first frost of winter in his hair, black brows arching over his eyes, he raised his hand and said, "Wusamequin, why do you sound your war cry?"

"British soldiers!" Wusamequin announced excitedly. "Not far from here! My spirit guide, Great Bear, is attacking them for me!"

There was a stir among the men. Excited smiles broke out. The dark eyes of his cousins gleamed with anticipation and eagerness. Then the women hurried up, having left their cook pots and wigwams. Some carried babies. Word was passed: Wusamequin's honor was about to be restored. Dogs yipped at the excitement and a baby began to yowl.

"Wusamequin!" A brave named Tashtassuck hurried toward the medicine man and clapped him on the shoulder. Few dared to touch the shaman in such a familiar way. "My heart soars at this news!"

Oneko smiled broadly. "The very day," he said, for of course he had remembered. He kept track of all the important events in the lives of his people. "Surely the spirits have delivered your enemies to you." He gestured to the men. "Go with your brother and help him fight his battle. Bring back many scalps to honor his good fortune. Wet your tomahawks in the blood of the Yangees!"

Now Odina stepped from among the women. She was carefully dressed in a deerskin dress with beaded, fringed sleeves. Her hair was arranged in two braids and adorned with feathers. Her dark eyes glistened with tears. "My heart soars for you, Wusamequin," she said huskily. "These deaths will heal your heart."

He didn't acknowledge her words. She was a woman, and this was man's business. Besides that, he didn't want her to think that his healed heart would be open to her. The death of his wife was a wound that would never heal.

"Great Sachem," he said to Oneko, "I have an obligation toward the welfare of the People of the River. I must warn you that if we fight the Yangees, there'll be blood shed by our men as well. The Yangees are well armed."

"Our men are brave and strong," Oneko replied, smiling encouragingly at the men, who were already telling their wives to fetch their weapons. "It'll be an honor for them to fight beside you."

"Then let's go," Tashtassuck said, "before even one Yangee gets away!"

The weapons were brought—tomahawks, war clubs, and flintlocks, a few pistols, and sharp scalping knives. The men painted their faces with blue and red from clay bowls. Oneko reached his hand into the bowl to paint Wusamequin's face, but the medicine man held up his hand.

"I'll wear ashes," he said.

Odina gazed at him, then looked down sadly, and Wusamequin wondered if she had seen the truth in his eyes: He would never become her husband. Then she left the crowd and disappeared from his sight.

The painting was completed in short order. The men arranged their weaponry.

Then Wusamequin raised his hands to bless the war party; he opened the medicine bag on his hip and extracted pollen and ground tobacco, which he flung over the heads of the warriors. The fragrant dust settled on their hair and clung to their paint.

They prepared to go. A high-pitched ululation rose among the women as they sang the men to battle. Squaws embraced their husbands. Tashtassuck's wife handed him an extra powder horn, which he slung over his neck and across his shoulder.

Odina returned, out of breath, and handed Wusamequin a scalping knife. He recognized it as her father's. Wopigwooit wasn't in the crowd; an aged elder, he suffered from the old people's disease and rarely left their wigwam.

"Wopigwooit sends it with his blessing," she told him.

There was a light in her eyes; he knew that she meant this act to be more than the loaning of a valuable weapon. He felt a moment's fleeting longing for the touch of a woman, the warmth of someone beside him at night. Perhaps he was being foolish and hasty; maybe once his blood feud was settled, his heart would soften toward her.

He sheathed the knife in the waistband of his breechcloth and turned to the men.

"Follow me!" he shouted. "My spirit will be freed this day!"

As the women sang them away, the men broke into a run, fierce and proud as eagles and wolves, powerful as bears.

Blood would be spilled.

*At last.*

# ❦ Chapter Four ❦

The sky had lightened somewhat, as if the eerie blackness had accompanied the massive brown bear. The great creature was no longer a menace. It had been shot several times, and now it lowed like a cow in its suffering. Heaving on its hind legs, it wobbled forward, then backward, and fell on its side.

The men of the 35th had proved their mettle. The fracas won, they were backing away from the wounded animal. Some had fixed their bayonets; as a result, many were sprayed with blood. Others pointed toward the lifting sky, talking and clapping one another on the back with relief.

"This'll be a story to tell our grandchildren!" one of the men said to another. His hair was bright red, and his smile was toothy and expansive.

Isabella half-lay across her saddle, gasping in her father's arms as his lips brushed the crown of her hair.

He gave her shoulders a squeeze and said, "Courage, poppet. It's over. I must see to the wounded."

"Papa," she ventured. "I need to ask you to help me with my lacings . . ."

But he didn't hear her. He set her firmly back on her horse and rode away. She gritted her teeth and shook her head as she raised an arm at his retreating back. He thought she had the vapors, like some fragile maid.

*It all comes from lack of air, not courage,* she thought with frustration.

The men were talking all at once, laughing and cleaning off their weapons. Major Whyte was hard put to secure their attention, and as she slid off her horse and wobbled toward the stream, he raised his pistol in the air and fired it.

"Enough!" he bellowed. "I will have your eyes and ears *now!*"

Seeing as it could be that he meant that literally, his troops immediately complied, even Ben Schoten, whose face was drenched with blood. Men were groaning; one was weeping. Surgeon Stevens knelt over a limp figure, muttering things to a soldier who knelt on one knee beside him to act as his assistant.

*If only he would listen, I would be able to help him myself,* she thought huffily.

Suddenly she heard the cawing of birds—or so it sounded at first to her. Then she covered her mouth with her glove, horror washing over her like the icy spray of the waterfall. Her horse began to panic, stomping its feet and throwing back its head.

*Those are the war cries of Indians!*

"Papa!" she cried.

The men had heard it, too, and Major Whyte was already issuing orders. They were reassembling in rows, becoming once more the fighting men of Britain.

"Look alive!" Major Whyte shouted. "Get the wounded into the forest! Reload your weapons!"

"Isabella!" her father cried from his place beside the injured soldier. "Savages! Run into the forest! Hide yourself!"

*Run?* she thought incredulously.

She took a step back toward her horse, thinking to remount. But the horse bolted. Isabella jumped away, then lost her balance and tumbled to the ground.

The shrieks grew louder.

"Fix bayonets!" Major Whyte shouted.

"Isabella!" Dr. Stevens cried again.

*I must do something!*

She flopped over on her hands and raised herself to her knees. Her right hand slid forward in the mud; she pulled back. And then her fingertips brushed something hard. A sharp pain sliced her palm and she would have cried out if she had been able to manage a sound.

She gripped her hand around the object and pulled it from the muck.

It was a knife. She had never seen it before, which meant that it probably did not belong to her father. She had no idea how it got there, but she was grateful for it nonetheless.

Closing her eyes, she wrapped both her hands around it, aimed it directly at her sternum, and brought it downward. She began to saw at the lacings of her corset, and gasped aloud when the first crisscross of dark green ribbons was severed. Upon the cutting of the second, she sucked in huge gulps of air. The third, and she carefully placed the knife between her teeth and yanked hard on the two sections of her corset.

Her rib cage finally freed, she inhaled like a drowning woman, spitting out her knife. She grabbed it up, still breathing hard; then she staggered to her feet and lifted her skirts—just as a figure leaped from the top of the waterfall and splashed into the water. She whirled around and tried to hold up her skirt with one hand as she gripped the knife with the other.

She was vaguely aware that she was screaming.

A wiry painted savage dressed in leather clothing crested the bubbling waters. As soon as he caught sight of her, he began slogging through the water straight for her. The water swirled around his thighs, then only to his knees as he advanced.

She screamed louder, backing away. She could not read his face, or his expression; he grinned like a devil in his warpaint. His hair was caught away from his face with feathers and he wore a silver earring; he held a tomahawk in one hand and a huge club in the other.

He said something in his native tongue, and then he stepped onto the bank of the stream. Dripping wet, his paint sliding down his features as if they were melting, he lunged at her.

She shrieked, "Papa!" and then rather than race away, she jumped straight at him, extending her knife. The sharp blade slashed his upper arm.

Her action startled him as much as it astonished her. His eyes widened and then he bolted toward her again. Staying her ground, she arced the knife, praying it would cut him again.

This time he stayed out of her reach, and her knife sliced at thin air as he began to circle around her.

Then a shot rang out. The savage's eyes widened and he shouted with pain. A bloom of crimson erupted on his leather shirt. He grabbed at it and lurched toward her, muttering at her in his heathen language.

Then he crumpled onto his knees and fell face first into the earth.

"Oh, thank God," Isabella moaned, catching her breath.

Just as another Indian leaped toward her from the top of the falls.

As he waded from the stream, Isabella turned and ran. She shouted, "Again! Fire again!" But the man who had saved her was busy reloading; her rescuer was none other than Ben Schoten.

She sent him a prayer of gratitude and kept running, heading for the forest. Her mind was flooded with terror. Her skirts dragged over the ground, catching on the exposed root of a pine tree: she stopped and yanked at it, then took the knife and hacked off the offending bit.

But it was too late.

Strong hands grabbed her around the waist. Then she and the Indian slammed to the ground, he landing on her. Her bones cracked and the wind was knocked out of her. She could not scream; she could only gasp; she saw stars as the world blurred into shades of gray and yellow.

Then he flipped her over on her back, and her fear snapped back her focus. She cowered at the wild look in his black, human eyes, which stared from circles of blue and black. Inhuman in visage, he smelled of blood and sweat. As he showed her his tomahawk, he grinned at her and grabbed her hair.

*Oh, my God, I'm going to die!* she thought. *He's going to scalp me!*

At that instant, the skies burst open and it began to rain. The savage was startled and looked up. The rest of his war paint sluiced off his skin and she was startled to see that he was a man perhaps her father's age.

She had no idea how she had managed to keep hold of her knife, but time stopped for her as she stared at his leather shirt. Then she thrust the blade into his chest with all the force she could muster.

Blood sprayed from the wound as the Indian shrieked more in anger than in pain. As he yanked the knife out of his chest, he backhanded her with his free hand. Her head snapped painfully to the left into fresh mud.

He grabbed her hair again.

She began to pummel his face and shoulders, kicking her legs in a frenzy as she worked to free herself. He laughed and grabbed her wrists with both his hands. Then he caught them both with his left hand as he spoke to her in his language. With his other hand he picked up her knife and showed it to her. Raindrops smacked the metal and slapped her face. His smile was cruel. He was playing with her, savoring her fear.

Thunder rumbled above them. Lightning flashed. A wind sailed over the man's body, stirring his long, wet hair in the rain, as if he were sitting on the bottom of the sea. Isabelle realized she could hear no gunshots, no screams. All she heard was the wind, and her own whimpering.

*Stop it, stop it*, she ordered herself. *You are the daughter of a British officer.*

But she could not stop it. She was bitterly afraid.

He drew the knife along the center of her face. Isabella remembered the stories she had heard of white women captured by savages and mutilated straight off, their nostrils slit as soon as they were captured. Her mind blurred ahead to when they were returned to their white families, and the sight of their shame had caused husbands to turn away and claim, "This is not my wife."

If such was to be her fate . . .

"No!" she shouted, baring her teeth like a feral animal. "You shall *not!*"

She twisted her head left, right, as the rain pelted it. Impatiently, he grabbed her chin and forced the back of her head flat against the mud. Water pooled in the hollow he had created, the rainwater rapidly pooling and trickling into her ears. He held her still and spoke to her, his eyes crinkling with laughter.

The rain poured through the cracked, wounded sky. Brusquely, he released her chin and yanked her hands back over her head. His fingers were rough against her smooth flesh, but he still had trouble holding onto her. His hands were slippery with his own blood.

Thunder rumbled; lightning answered. A zigzag of yellow light slashed across his face, giving him the look of a gargoyle in an engraving of an old French church in her father's Bible.

*He is from hell*, she thought wildly. *He's a fiend.*

Lightning flashed again, and he dipped his head toward her loose, drenched bodice. The two torn panels had separated, and though she was still covered, it was only in the broadest sense of the word.

The brave smiled in the way of men who are thinking of indecent things. The shadows and planes of his face shifted. He narrowed his lids; his voice dropped to a husky whisper. He moved against her . . .

. . . and she realized that now he had a different sort of torment in mind for her.

"No!" she screamed. "Papa! *Papa!*"

She bucked beneath him, trying to bite his hand as it held her wrists, writhing and rocking to force him off her body. Her efforts were clumsy and useless; her skirts and heavy petticoats were soaked through with rain. She felt like a prisoner in irons, shackled by the sodden layers of fabric.

He reached down to move the ruined corsetry away from her stomach. His rough fingertips painted her skin with cold red dye that the downpour diluted and smeared, so that it looked as if he had stabbed her.

Goosebumps raised on her wet skin; she felt a sharp moment of despair, and then, without thinking, she sucked saliva into her mouth and spit at him.

He blinked, and then he guffawed as the spittle smacked against his left cheek and began to run down his chin with the rainwater.

Isabella screamed at him, "No!"

He laughed harder. The thunder roared like cannonballs; lightning stabbed the clouds and the trees, illuminating them like bonfires.

As he wiped the spittle away, he reached down to touch her again. She drew away, pressing her head into the mud, closing her eyes, and wishing herself dead rather than this. He snickered at her. Her fear amused him.

Then a sharp voice rang over his laughter. The man jerked and looked up, and spoke back, chuckling and gesturing to Isabella.

Isabella tried to turn her head, but she could only shift her eyes to the left. All she could see were a pair of bloody, dirt-encrusted moccasins and leather leggings caught up with leather thongs at the knees. The leggings were fringed, the moccasins decorated with colorful quills.

The moccasins drew closer as their owner snapped at her captor. Her attacker's merriment faded. He shook his head and glanced down at Isabella, speaking of her as he gestured to himself.

The other man spoke again and walked toward Isabella.

His face rigid with anger, Isabella's captor pushed his face toward hers, hissing like a snake. Then he sat back on his heels and rose to a standing position. He shook his knife at her, whirled on his heel, and stomped away.

Painfully, she turned her head and found the owner of the bloody moccasins.

She could not breathe.

He was very tall, and his hair was a deep blue-black, slicked away from his face and forehead by the rain. His brows were arched above dark, fathomless eyes. His face was sharply chiseled, with flared cheekbones and deep hollows in his cheeks, then a square jaw with a dimple in the center. The rain washed across his straight nose, and his lips parted as he stared back at her.

He stopped walking and stood shirtless, his chest slathered with blood and war paint. His breechcloth rode low on his hips; leggings were tied around his sinewy thighs and at his knees. He had long legs and long arms, and in his right hand he held a knife.

There was blood on the blade.

She scrabbled away from him; he hurried toward her, transferring his knife to his left hand and showing her his empty right palm. She shook her head wordlessly.

He said to her, "*Mahwah.*"

It was the voice.

Soft in her ear, the voice she had heard whispering through the forest.

She cleared her throat, but no sound came out. She tried again to move away from him, slipping in the mud.

He glided easily to her side and grabbed her wrist. He smelled of smoke. He braced himself and pulled her up, grinning faintly as she tried to ensure that her body was shielded from his gaze while at the same time keeping her balance.

Then all thought of herself fled as she caught sight of the scene behind him.

The gallant soldiers of the 35th lay sprawled in pools of blood. Arms, legs, chests gushed with blood. None moved.

As she surveyed the scene in mute horror, she caught sight of Ben Schoten's still form. She reeled in shock at the sight of the bloody circle atop his head.

He had been scalped.

Many of the fallen had lost their hair. As she stumbled backward in mute horror, a brave loped over to another body, grabbed up a fistful of straw-colored hair, raised a wickedly glinting knife over his head, and hacked the hair off, bringing flesh with it.

She covered her mouth with both hands. She swayed and would have fallen if the brave had not pulled her toward him by the wrist and crushed her against his chest.

She made no sound, only panted in shock. He held her against his body without speaking, cupping the crown of her head so that she couldn't peer around his shoulder. They stood in the rain as Isabella fought not to go mad from what she had just witnessed. She clung to him, aware that he was one of *them*, and yet not able to let go.

The lightning flashed overhead; she heard a strange groaning that reminded her of the great brig that had transported her parents and her to this terrible place. An ear-splitting crack followed, and then a huge crash.

He held her tightly and spoke in his language. It was the voice.

*Isabella . . .*

She took refuge in it, not so much listening as hanging onto it, knowing that if she stopped listening she would go mad.

Then she felt him moving his left arm. She tried to lift her head but he kept her cradled against his chest with her right hand. He spoke again, in a sort of chant.

The rain stopped immediately.

He let go of her head and she glanced up at the sky as she stepped away from him. The storm clouds scudded across the sky like a V of passenger pigeons. A scarlet sun blazed through, casting the forest in beams of crimson, as if there weren't enough red already—blood on bloodred coats; two dozen men slaughtered like animals . . .

She took another step away as the Indian warriors rushed up to the two of them, encircling them. Their faces were wet with blood.

She said to him, "Where is my father, you filthy murderer?"

He stared hard at her, shadows shifting across the angles and planes of his face.

She tried again. "My fa—"

"Father," he repeated. He turned to one of the other Indians. They spoke for a moment. Then five of the men left the circle and dashed into the forest.

He said to Isabella, "Father."

No one else spoke or moved. Raindrops trickled off the leaves of the trees. The waterfall rushed and roared. Her heart pounded so hard she was afraid it would burst from her chest.

"If you've hurt him . . ." Her voice shook; she twisted her hands together, her nails pressing into her palms so hard she drew blood. His face remained impassive as his glance ticked from her to the place where the men had disappeared.

He moved away—to tend, she saw, the savage who had first attacked her. He chanted over him, and opened up some sort of heathen pouch, pulling out various objects. She couldn't quite make out what he was doing. Possibly he was praying to the Devil.

The other began to speak conversationally among

themselves; then one grabbed up a leather thong and showed it to the man next to him.

Three fresh scalps fluttered from the thong. The hair of men who had been alive only moments ago, men who had marched through the forest in her company. Men with bright red coats and shiny buttons; nursery soldiers.

She wanted to scream. She wanted to run.

*I mustn't panic. I have to keep my wits about me.*

There was a shout. Isabella and the tall man both turned their heads in its direction at the same time. There was a rustling in the thick underbrush; then two of the Indians reappeared from a thick copse of trees. One of them, a rather fleshy man, was holding a hemp-colored rope. As he stepped through the brush, he stopped and tugged on it.

Her father staggered into view. The other end of the rope was tied around his neck. His face was drenched with blood and one eye was swollen shut. But he was alive.

And he had his hair.

"Papa!" she cried. She pushed through the circle of savages and raced to his side. Carefully she raised on tiptoe and placed her arms around his neck. The Indian who held the rope tugged on it, forcing her father to stumble. Isabella turned her head toward the savage and shouted, "Leave him alone!"

All the braves laughed, except for Isabella's rescuer. He stared at her with his dark, unblinking eyes. A muscle jumped in his cheek. Then he left the circle and walked toward her. As he drew near, she held onto her father.

"No!" she screamed at him, then at the others. "No! Don't touch him!"

"Poppet," her father rasped through cracked and bleeding lips. "Do not provoke them."

"Leave us alone!" she railed at the tall, handsome man. "Leave us!"

The man held up his empty weapon hand. He said gently to her, "Father lives."

"You speak English!" she cried. Relief swept through her. "Then certainly you are civilized." She bobbed a curtsey, though she had to force herself to bend her knee to these barbarians, who had butchered over two dozen men. "Sir, we are on a mission of mercy. We carry medicines to men who are very ill. We—"

"Silence," he snapped. Then he turned on his heel. His back to her, he rejoined the cluster of men.

"Sir!" she called after him. "I beg of you! Allow me to parlay with you!"

He ignored her. As she stared after him, the circle broke up and the men began to amble down the path.

She took up her station beside her father. She held onto his torn uniform coat like a child clinging to a cloth doll. They stumbled through the mud. She was dizzy and sick with fear.

"My dear, did they harm you?" her father murmured under his breath. He scrutinized her, frowning with dismay. "Your cheek bears a bruise."

"The tall one, he saved me." Then she caught sight of the Indian who had struck her and said, "That one, he . . . he was no gentleman." She choked back a sob and added hastily, "But I am all right, Papa."

"These monsters. We carried a flag of truce," he spat. "They shall pay, by God."

"Papa . . . is everyone else . . . did anyone survive?" she asked, darting a glance at the carnage in the glade. She thought of Ben Schoten, scalped and bloody, and felt her gorge rise afresh. "If there are wounded, perhaps they will allow me to care for them."

"That's not the Indian way," he said harshly. "If they meant to take any man prisoner, he would be with us already." He looked away. "Three warriors remained behind when they took me, and they are dispatching the wounded now."

"Oh, Papa," she groaned. "Oh, dear heaven."

"Courage, girl," he urged her. "While we are alive, we have hope."

"Papa, to kill wounded men . . ." She was near speechless from this new horror.

"It is the way of war, sometimes." His face hardened. "Not the British way, however."

She swallowed and tried to nod. Her knees were rubbery. Her body felt uncommonly light, as if she had left it.

"I did see some men take to the forest," he added, with a note of hope. "I can only pray they will make their way to Fort William Henry, and alert Colonel

Ramsland of our plight. But the Indians have sent men after them. Of that I'm certain."

"Was Major Whyte among them?" she asked.

"Aye." Her father's voice was sharp. "He was one who . . . ran."

For a moment she was so shocked she couldn't speak. "You mean . . . he *deserted* us?"

He clamped shut his mouth, which was answer enough. Her father was not one to speak ill of anyone, least of all a fellow officer. She thought of how Major Whyte had looked at her; it was nearly impossible to conceive that he could have left her to die.

"What is to become of us?" she asked brokenly.

"Trust in God, my dear," her father answered gently. He lowered his head. "He will deliver us from evil."

She closed her eyes. "Amen."

The Indian who was leading her father jerked on the rope, and Dr. Stevens staggered forward. Isabella grabbed his bound hand and tried to help him.

"*Mahwah.*"

It was the tall brave. He had stopped walking; his body shifted toward her, he gestured at her with his hand.

"Do as he says, girl," her father urged her. "Don't move him to anger."

"I have no wish to be parted from you." Her voice cracked with anxiety.

"Nor I you." His glance ticked from her to the tall Indian. He took a breath and said, "But be obedient to him. I sense that you are his personal captive.

Their customs are different than ours, Isabella." His cheeks reddened; his eyes broke contact. "According to their traditions, he may . . . he may do with you as he pleases."

"*Papa*," she said, stricken.

He took a ragged breath. "He speaks English. It may be that he's a gentleman." Then he turned back to her and said, "You know that I would die rather than see you harmed in any way."

"Please, no, I beg of you," she said, taking his hand and putting it against her cheek. Her blue eyes spilled with tears. "Please, Papa, don't speak of dying. I couldn't bear it. I'm so fearful, Papa."

"I shan't go without a fight," he assured her. "Remember, Isabella. We are British. We must behave like civilized people." He stared at the tall, handsome man. "Even if others do not."

# ⁂ Chapter Five ⁂

What shall I do with her? Wusamequin wondered. And why have I spared her and her father? All the others that we could kill, we have killed. The ones who ran are being hunted down and put to the blade.

*My family is avenged, and I may walk with honor through the village. I am Wusamequin, medicine man of the People of the River. Now my wife and son will leave the Land Beyond and walk the Road of Stars.*

He gazed up at the sky.

*Where the Road of Stars will take them, I cannot know for sure. But I do know it will be a more wonderful place than even the Land Beyond. They will dance with the spirits. They will become spirits.*

*I have accomplished my deeds this day, for them. My life as a man and as a warrior is redeemed.*

*The price was light. Tashtassuck was wounded, but only by shot. He is able to walk home. But Great Bear, walking in this world, was slaughtered. I should kill these two for his sake. Why do I stay my hand?*

Why had he stopped Sasious from savoring the spoils of victory?

*It was her courage. She fought like a woman of my people,*

54

*not a weak Yangee. I could not let her spirit be shamed.*

He shook his head. Now who was being weak?

He glanced at Sasious, who had a shallow flesh wound from the white skin woman's knife. He was glowering from the insult.

*I have probably made an enemy. That was foolish of me.*

He scanned overhead, seeking signs. A hawk wheeled in the newly cleansed heavens. Passenger pigeons fluttered away, warning one another of the threat.

Two deer paused in the underbrush as he and Sasious led the party toward the cliff where, twenty feet behind them, the waterfall rushed and burbled. Three moons ago—Buck Moon—he had had a dream that told him that upon occasion, his wife visited him in the world wearing the guise of a deer. Perhaps the second deer was his son, whose name he also did not mention, in order to ensure his easy journey on the Road of Stars.

He signed greetings and love to them. The two deer calmly watched, then turned tail and trotted into the forest.

The white woman beside him watched their progress as well.

Sasious started up the steep path that had been cut into the cliff. Wusamequin paused, indicating that the woman should go ahead of him. She hesitated, then did so, looking behind to catch sight of her father. After she assured herself that the grayhair was still there, she took the first foothold. He could see her exhaustion and admired her attempts to conceal it. He admired her pride.

He watched her body move as she climbed the steep incline. She was wearing the odd forms beneath her skirt that mocked her womanly shape, flaring out her hips so that she looked like a bizarre sort of duck. The clothes of the Yangees were ridiculous. They trussed their women into walking prisons—to no purpose that he could see, save to emphasize their indolence and uselessness. White skin women were like badly made pieces of pottery—garishly painted but created too poorly to be of value.

The men, too, wore so many clothes that they could neither run nor work with any ease of movement. They spent inordinate amounts of time either caring for their clothing, or working to earn wampum to purchase more. It was madness.

He scowled. It was a madness his own people had caught. Until the white skins came, the People had made all their own clothes, their weapons, and their household necessities. Now they traded for these things, and the People were beginning to forget how to make them. They had grown soft and foolish, dependent on the Yangees and *les Français*.

His anger flared, and he gripped his tomahawk. The white skins were murdering his people in so many ways. Better that they all be put to death.

He stared at her back, watching the muscles work beneath the frayed fabric. For the sake of her modesty, she had wound strips of outer garment over her ruined clothing. He was moved. He was not an ignorant man; he was aware that the world was a vast place, and he was tolerant of many of the white skins' customs. She needed to cover herself in this way to walk in the Way of her people.

But the white skins were not tolerant of any departure from their way of doing things. They judged others' ways with disdain and sought to stamp out anything that did not come from them. They were arrogant and dangerous, like a young brave overcome with rum. The Indians who lived in All-ba-nee had reported at last year's potlach that the Yangees were fond of saying, "The only good Indian is a dead Indian."

He felt shame for having prevented Sasious from ravishing her. The war leader had been humiliated and for what? A white woman.

*She is one of them. She is my enemy.*

After they reached the top of the cliff, Wusamequin surveyed the scene below. So many dead. So much blood. Let the vultures and wolves devour the flesh and defile the hearts of the dead Yangees. It pleased him.

Ninigret moved up beside him. He clapped a hand on Wusamequin's shoulder and said, "My heart soars for you." Then he tilted his head, studying the shaman. "Something is not well with you, my brother. What more can you need today? Your family honor has been restored."

Wusamequin said nothing.

Ninigret said thoughtfully, "Tashtassuck will recover?"

"Yes."

"And your family . . . is it that the memories do not want to leave you?"

"They wish to haunt me," Wusamequin agreed.

"We will sit in the sweat lodge with you and force them to depart," Ninigret offered. "After we have killed the prisoners." His smile returned. "It was wise of you to save captives for the women and the elders. They have need of vengeance as well. The massacre affected all of us. Our dead brother and sister were much loved."

"Yes." Wusamequin considered Ninigret's words. He spoke truth.

The war party continued the trek back to the village. The white captives were tiring; it took many jerks on the rope to force the grayhair to keep up. The woman's gaze had taken on the dazed expression of those pushed beyond their endurance. She walked like a ghost, and he was sorry. He missed her fire.

The familiar scent of cooking pots told him he was near home. The war band walked past the women's fields of corn, ready for harvest. The village dogs bounded toward the warriors, yipping and leaping on them, overjoyed to see them. Wusamequin's tame wolf, Afraid-of-Everything, nuzzled his master's hand, licking off the blood—both Wusamequin's own and that of his enemies. He caught the girl staring at the wolf in horror. Then she turned and silently retched.

Wearing his ceremonial blanket, Oneko met the party at the boundary of the village. He held a coup stick and he regarded Wusamequin with pride. There was sorrow, too, for the one who had died.

As he surveyed the two prisoners with a cold gaze, he said, "Wusamequin, are you avenged? Did your tomahawk drink the blood of Yangee soldiers this day?"

Wusamequin held his head high. "Yes, great Sachem." He gestured to the collections of scalps that fluttered against the leggings of the warriors. "You will hear us count coup at the fire tonight. Tashtassuck has a wound, but he is well."

Oneko smiled broadly. "My heart soars for all of you. This is a wonderful boon for the *keutikaw* of your family." He gestured to the bloody group of men. "Now go to the sweat lodge and purge death from yourselves. Don't bring death into our village." He glanced at the captives. "Although we will happily kill these two at our fires tonight."

Wusamequin said nothing. But as he turned to accompany the other men to the sweat lodge, located in a clearing on the village outskirts, he heard the white woman call after him in a voice filled with fear and despair.

"Sir! Sir, I beg of you! Do not leave us!"

Though his heart urged him to turn to her, give her some gesture of reassurance, he made no effort to respond. She was the slave, not he.

And most likely, she would be dead by morning.

*Unless I receive a sign to spare her. If I do spare her, her life will belong to my people, and she will be a slave until the day she dies.*

"For the love of God, help us!" she shouted.

The girl had fallen to the ground, and she was curling into a ball and covering her head as Oneko's wife, Wabun-Anung, delivered a sharp kick to her ribs. The grayhair, sprawled beside her, was bleeding from a fresh blow to the head.

So the taunting of the condemned had begun.

"Great Sachem!" he called to Oneko.

His chief glanced from the spectacle to the medicine man.

"Yes, Wusamequin?"

"We need to ask the white skins about the plans of the Yangees," he reminded Oneko. "Where they were going and why. We need to keep the prisoners alive and able to speak until that time."

Sasious spat on the ground beside Wusamequin.

"Why bother? They'll only lie. That's all the white skin devils know how to do. Lie. Better to kill them and be done with it. Tonight is the *keutikaw*, the great feast to mark the passage of thirteen moons, when we will end the mourning of your dead loved ones. It's fitting they should die tonight."

Oneko looked from Sasious to Wusamequin. Wusamequin saw the glimmer of interest in his eyes; the great chief knew that bad blood simmered between the two of them.

Wusamequin had not understood the woman's

barrage of Yangee words. She had spoken too fast. That was no source of shame to him; he spoke more English than any other tribal member. In the days when things were better between the People and the Yangee, he had spent a lot of time with a Yangee trapper named James Anderson. James Anderson had taught him English, even shown him many of the markings that were used to record thoughts. The People used beaded belts in the same way as James Anderson's "papers," and Wusamequin wished he could have learned James Anderson's Way before they had separated.

Oneko said, "Sasious speaks truth. We were once great friends with the Yangee. We believed his words and treated him as a brother. And the People of the River have suffered terribly for that trust. The Yangee told us he was our friend. And then he killed your wife and son, Wusamequin."

The Sachem gestured to the prisoners. The young woman had thrown herself on top of her father's still form and was kicking out at anyone who tried to come close enough to harm him. This had set most of the village to laughing—an indication of their admiration for her courage—and she was screaming at them with English words he had never heard before.

She had balled her fists and was punching at the air, crying and shrieking like the winter wind. What was left of her dress was in shreds, but she gave no thought to her once-treasured modesty. Her fury reminded her of the vengeful protection of Great Bear. The death of such a woman would be a loss . . .

unless she lived to bear Yangee sons.

Then her death would be welcome.

"What a wild thing," Oneko said approvingly as he watched her.

"She won't even burn well," Sasious hissed. "There's no fat on her. The Yangee have starved her."

There was an angry cut above her eye and a scratch on her cheek.

*I'd use monarda—bee balm—and pollen on that,* Wusamequin found himself thinking. He was looking at her with a healer's eye. But if she burned tonight at the fire, what need was there to dress her wounds?

It took Wusamequin a moment to realize that Oneko was studying him. Warmth touched his face as he looked questioningly at the tribal leader. Oneko was smiling.

"Very well, medicine man," he said. "We shall make sure the prisoners are able to answer questions. Now go to the sweat lodge. You carry death with you." He raised his voice. "All of you, purify yourselves!"

Sasious hefted his tomahawk as he turned away from Oneko and Wusamequin. The medicine man began to turn as well, but Oneko said, "What has happened between you?" He glanced over his shoulder. "Was it the woman? Does she plead with your heart?"

"She is a Yangee," Wusamequin declared. "Nothing more."

"After you have gone to the sweat lodge, come to my wigwam and talk to me. I have things to say to you." Oneko adjusted his blanket around his shoulders. His hair was turning white; he was becoming a very old man. In the Way of the People, elders were revered above all else. The world was difficult; it required not only physical strength, but skill and wisdom to live a long life.

Wusamequin included his head. "I will."

He cast another glance at the woman and her father. The laughter of the People had grown so intense that some of the squaws were doubled over. Afraid-of-Everything was prancing among the children, licking at fingers and searching for treats.

"I will put the captives away, where they will be safe," Oneko drawled. "And we will talk."

Wusamequin drew himself up. He said coolly, "They're of no interest to me, Great Sachem Oneko. With your permission, I'll be on my way."

Oneko reached out a hand, but he didn't touch Wusamequin's contaminated flesh. It was the way of the People to avoid contact with those who had killed, until the death was washed away.

"Today's a day filled with joy for you, and with sorrow, too. Hatred has lived in your heart for a long time. It will leave a hole in your heart that still must be healed. You are our medicine man. You know this to be true."

"I do," Wusamequin replied.

"Do not fill your heart with a bad spirit," Oneko continued. "It will not stay empty long, if you walk your path well. It will heal now that you have fulfilled your vow." He smiled kindly at the younger man. "Go with your brothers, who love you."

He gestured meaningfully at the retreating Sasious. "Give your brother a gift, something you treasure. Let him know that you value his friendship."

It was a wise suggestion. Wusamequin felt his features soften. Oneko was the closest thing Wusamequin had to father or uncle; his blood elders were dead.

"I will."

Oneko smiled at him. "Remember who you are, young shaman. You are more than just another brave. You are our spirit warrior. It is a strong thing to walk side by side with you. Those who believe themselves cast away from you will feel weaker for the loss of your company. That will frighten them.

"Frightened men do what they must to feel stronger." Oneko sighed heavily. "The People are very frightened, Wusamequin. We have been weakened by the white skins. We must form strong bonds of brotherhood among ourselves."

"I understand you," Wusamequin said.

Oneko pointed to the scalp knife in his hand. "That would be a fine gift. That's an exquisite weapon."

Wusamequin shook his head. "It's not mine to give. It belongs to Odina's father, Wopigwoot."

Oneko grinned slyly at his shaman. "Wopigwoot would be happy if it were carried by a son-in-law. And a son-in-law would have the right to give it to whomever he pleased." He crinkled his eyes and pursed his lips, and he looked like a grizzled old turtle.

He continued, "We are few, and the white skins are many. We must have children, Wusamequin. You're a young man. Vigorous. You can put many sons in the belly of a wife. You need to take a new wife. If she is still in the Land Beyond, your wife understands that. Soon she will walk the Road of Stars, and she will let this world go."

"I . . ." Wusamequin bowed his head, not wishing to think of that in this moment. "Oneko, I . . ."

"Don't stutter," Oneko said, feinting a box to Wusamequin's ear. "Go and wash yourself. I don't like to stand so close to death."

Wusamequin hesitated. Oneko blew out a sigh and called to the squaws and children, "Gather up the white skins. We will put them away for now."

Cheers and laughter rose from the throng as Odina and her sister, Keshkecho, darted toward the white woman and tried to grab her arms. The woman lunged at them, her teeth bared, swiping at them with her hands. Odina laughed shrilly and bent down to her side. She picked up a small rock and hefted it in her hand, preparing to take aim—

"No!" Oneko called to her. "Just put them away." To Wusamequin, he said, "Does that satisfy you?"

The medicine man crossed his hands over his chest. "I told you, the white skins are not my concern."

With that, he left for the sweat lodge.

# ❖ Chapter Six ❖

Surrounded by screaming women, laughing children, and barking, wolflike dogs, Isabella struggled as two of the Indian women grabbed her wrists and hoisted her to her feet. "No!" she shrieked, kicking at them and yanking her arms as hard as she could. "Papa!"

She pushed herself against the ground to give herself the momentum to look back at her father as she was pulled along. Not far behind her, he was being half-lifted, half-dragged by six or seven women, almost like a man in his coffin carried aloft by his pall bearers. His head drooped over the shoulder of an ancient crone. She said something and the others burst into a flurry of giggles.

Then they were herded toward a small circular building constructed of saplings and bark. She thought of the cairns of Ireland, hillocks in which Celtic kings were buried. For a moment, terror got the best of her—was this to be her tomb?—and then she gathered her wits about herself again. It had to mean something that they hadn't been killed in the forest. Unless the Indians simply wanted to share the pleasure of butchering Englishmen with their families.

She was surprised at how little she knew of the ways of the Indians. She had never actually touched an Indian before. She had lived in the Colonies for almost a year, and yet she couldn't speak even a single word of their language.

"There is no need, my dear, to speak their tongue," Mrs. DeWitt had once commented. "After all, they need to learn English, if they are to make their way in the new order of things. Their languages will die out, and a fine thing that is, too. It's all gibberish and prevents them from progressing, don't you know."

*If only I could speak one word. Just one. Perhaps they would understand that I mean no harm. That I am just a frightened girl.*

The prettier of her two captors spoke roughly to her and gestured toward the hut. Then a much younger girl raced to the hut and pulled back the flap. She gestured excitedly for Isabella to be taken inside. The two women who held her arms started speaking in higher, more excited voices.

"Papa!" She strained to reach him, pushing the hand of the pretty woman away as she worked her arm free. She lurched forward, crying, "Please, he is a physician! Do any among you have wounds? Diseases? He can heal you!"

A little boy trotted up beside her and swatted her on the thigh with a stick. Despite the layers of mud-caked petticoats that served as protective layers between her flesh and his weapon, the blow still hurt. When she yelped, he giggled at her and scampered away.

"We came in peace," she said brokenly. "Will no one listen to me? I am . . . I am . . ."

And then she heard the voice inside her head, the one that had carried on the wind.

His voice, saying "*Mahwah.*"

She said it aloud. "*Mahwah.*"

The pretty woman beside her jerked her head toward her. Isabella's eyes widened with hope that she had at last distracted her from her single-minded cruelty.

"*Mahwah,*" Isabella repeated.

"*Mahwah,*" the woman echoed, looking mildly shocked. Then she spoke to the other woman, who was rather plain and quite plump, and the two looked back at Isabella.

"*Mahwah,*" Isabella said again.

The plain woman spoke to the pretty woman, and they both laughed. Then the pretty one yanked hard on Isabella's rose-shaped earbob. It would have ripped through her earlobe except that the hanger broke in the woman's grasp.

"Ow!" Isabella cried.

The woman danged it in front of Isabella's face. "*Mahwah,*" she said, and placed the earbob into a small leather pouch back at her waist.

"Please, take the other one as well," Isabella urged,

unfastening it from her ear. She held it out to the woman, who snatched it from her and tossed it lazily to her companion. Then she sneered at Isabella and flicked her forefinger against Isabella's cheek, as if to say, *I may do whatever I wish to you.*

Then her father's convoy reached the front of the hut; the flap was raised and they tossed him inside as if he were a cord of wood. The pretty woman glared at her with a look of triumph. Then she half-led, half-dragged Isabella toward the flap, which was still being held up by a very old woman who had no teeth. Isabella could see nothing beyond it; the interior of the hut was pitch dark.

The pretty woman sneered at her and said, *"Mahwah!"* Then she drove Isabella into the hut, pushing her with all her strength.

Isabella stumbled in the darkness and nearly fell over her father, who was lying on the floor.

The flap dropped unceremoniously back into place.

"Papa," Isabella said, feeling for him. "Papa!" She was touching his face, her fingers running across his forehead. It was sticky and wet.

"I . . . I'm all right, poppet," he said hoarsely.

"What is happening? What are they doing?"

"I'm not certain." His voice was strained. He coughed hard.

"You're lying to me," she accused him. "Please, Papa, tell me what is to become of us."

"I . . ." He sighed. "My impression is that they

mean to . . ." He cleared his throat. "You are very young and beautiful. It may be that one of the men will . . . marry you."

"*Marry* me?" Her words were shrill. "That's not what you really mean, is it, Papa?"

"They are not Christians," he reminded her. "They do not follow Christian practices."

"They do not marry, then."

"Not as we do, no."

"They do not marry. And they cut the hair off living men." She choked back her sobs. "They murder men savagely. They butchered our escort and dispatched our wounded. Why have we been spared thus far?"

"I cannot say, girl. Perhaps they realized that I was an officer." He groaned. "Isabella, my hands are bound. Please see if you can untie them."

"Oh! I'm sorry," she blurted, fumbling to find his wrists. He was lying on them; she eased him gently onto his side and started feeling the thick rope, trying to locate the knot.

"Have you anything sharp?" he asked.

"No, I haven't," she said, frustrated and frightened. She worked at the rope. Her fingers were bleeding and sore, and the fibers of the rope jabbed like pins.

"Keep trying," he urged her. "Or perhaps you can find something on the ground. A piece of broken pottery."

"Yes, Papa." She raised up on her hands and knees,

feeling the earth. She remembered the knife she had found in the mud. That had seemed miraculous. Perhaps she would be so blessed a second time.

But after a few minutes' searching, she said despondently, "Papa, I have found nothing." She choked back a sob. "I'm so sorry!"

"It's not your fault, my girl," he assured her. "Now, listen, Isabella. We mustn't give up hope. We must pray and stay alert. We must escape if we have the chance. If you see an opportunity to run, you must leave me behind. Do you understand me?"

"I would never do that!" she shot back as she came to him and put her arms around his neck. "Never in a century, Papa!"

"You must, if you have the chance. And . . . and I shall do the same, Isabella. If one of us can reach civilization, we can summon help for the other."

"All . . . all right," she murmured, though she didn't honestly believe that her father would desert her, as Major Whyte had done.

"Good." His voice was firm and steady, filled with authority. "So that is our plan."

"Our . . . plan?" She was incredulous, but fought to hide it. That was no plan. "How shall we accomplish it?"

"We can hope that Providence will provide. Now help me up to a sitting position," he told her. "I don't want them to find me lying here trussed like a deer when they come to check on us."

"Indeed not," she said. It was awkward, but she accomplished it at last, easing him upright until he found his balance.

Then there was a sound like heavy fabric being torn. Isabella glanced fearfully in the direction of the flap, which was being lifted up.

A man stood in the opening to the hut. It was the brave who had attacked her, and he was carrying a torch. He was clean and he wore fresh clothing of beaded, fringed leather. His face was clear of paint, and he was an evil-looking man, with brows that tapered diagonally from his nose to his temples, and a hooked nose. His lips were thin and mean.

He gestured toward Isabella, indicating that she should come to him.

"Oh, Papa," she murmured, her eyes huge. Her face prickled with fear. "Papa, help me."

"Be strong, Isabella." His voice caught. "I love you, my daughter."

She stared at the man, so frightened that she couldn't remember how to move. Her corset was no longer an impediment. It had been such a ruin that she had cast it off as they had walked here. For the first time she realized how skimpily dressed she was, and how cold the air had grown. She was shivering violently, but she had been unaware of it.

The Indian gestured again and spoke gruffly to her.

She licked her lips and was about to say her single word in his language, "*Mahwah.*"

But someone said it before she could.

"*Mahwah.*"

It was the tall, handsome man, the one who had saved her. He appeared beside a man Isabella guessed was the tribe's leader, an older man with a distinguished bearing, for all of his being a savage, standing at his side. The chief was elaborately dressed, with several feathers twined into his long hair, and two beaded earbobs in his ear. Her rescuer wore a leather jerkin that had been decorated with dyed porcupine quills in purple and red. It stretched across his broad chest and tapered to his hips. He wore leggings and moccasins as before, and a breechcloth.

His hair had been arranged so that it was caught up at the crown of his head and allowed to cascade over his shoulders. He wore a silver earring and a cuff around his wrist.

Isabella's ravisher moved toward her; she shrank back against her father. His eyes narrowed; then he moved past her and he gripped her father's arm.

In turn, the tall man wrapped his fingers around Isabella's forearm. His face was very grim, and he wouldn't look at her. She could feel the muscles of his hand through her threadbare sleeve, and she realized that he was very strong.

The leader spoke and her attacker answered; then he laughed and said something in a mocking voice to Isabella's father.

It was then that she realized the chief was staring at the locket around her neck.

She touched it, murmured, "Oh, no." It was the only likeness of her mother in the Colonies; she could not bear to part with it.

But he continued to gaze at it. Swallowing, she reached up and tried to untie the velvet ribbon. But she was shaking too hard. Her fingers kept slipping at the knot.

The tall man turned to her, his dark eyes somber, his manner very grave. His hands slid behind her neck. His gaze bored into her as he worked the ribbon, his fingers brushing her neck. They were calloused, and rough. She could feel his body heat. Smell smoke and herbs on his skin.

His breath wafted over her face as he finally untied the ribbon. He drew it away, cupping the locket in his palm, and handed it to the chief. The man examined it for a moment. Then he pried the two halves open and saw the miniature of her mother.

He raised a brow and showed it to the man, saying, "*Mahwah.*"

"No, that's my mother," she said. "My mother. Not me."

"*Mahwah,*" the chief insisted, placing the locket around his neck as, with a gesture to the two younger men, he turned to leave. The two followed, each with his captive in tow.

"Sir, please, what is happening?" Isabella asked her rescuer. Was he still her rescuer? "Where are you taking us?"

He remained silent.

As they moved away from the hut, a yellow glow off to the right shone on the tall man's face. He was young. Certainly not as young as she, but she would have thought him too young to hold such a position of authority in his village. But then, she was thinking by British standards. For all she knew, he had won his rank by assassinating the man who had held it before him.

They walked on a few more steps, and then her father murmured, "Oh, dear Lord."

The man herded her to the left of another circular structure, and she saw what her father had seen: the villagers were thronged around a bonfire the height of three men, which blazed and crackled, smoke rising toward the moon. To the left of the fire but not so very far away, two tree-trunk posts stood upright. Piles of branches were heaped around them.

"Papa?" Isabella asked, her voice rising. He seemed to have aged ten years in the last minute. His face was haggard, his lids heavy. It was almost as if he had been drugged.

"Stay strong, Isabella," he said. "All is not yet lost."

"Oh, my God, Papa, do they mean to burn us?"

"Stay strong," he said again. "Remember that you

have a Redeemer in Heaven, who awaits your Christian soul."

The five of them walked toward the circle. A woman turned and saw them, and began to make a strange, unearthly cry with her mouth. The woman beside her joined in. Then a man.

A drum began to pound. Another.

*I will not die this day,* Isabella told herself, shaking violently. *I will not. The tall man will save me a second time.*

She looked over at him to reassure herself. But when he stared back at her, his face was hard as stone.

# ❖ Chapter Seven ❖

Silhouetted against the blazing fire, women broke from the circle and ran toward Isabella and her father. Isabella recognized the pretty woman who had taken her earbob as she raced up to Isabella and spat at her.

Isabella looked up at the tall man. His face was still hard.

"Please, sir," she said softly. "Help us."

He did not look at her as he said, "Silence."

By the time the five reached the circle, they were surrounded by screaming women. The drumbeats were feverish. Men were chanting.

Her father was led to the first of the two posts. Two men threw ropes to the evil-looking man, who began to wrap her father to the post. He made no struggle, but stood resolutely, his chin raised, his eyes open and clear. He was British to the core, and Isabella was moved by his heroism. She resolved that if they were both to die tonight, she would prove as illustrious an example of British courage as he.

But tears trickled down her cheeks. She couldn't imagine a worse fate than this.

Then the chief moved toward the prisoners and

spread forth his hands. He began to speak. The villagers immediately grew silent. A dog barked, yelped, made no more noise.

The tall man came up to Isabella. He gazed at her and said, "Oneko says, sell you to *les Français*."

"Sell us?" she whispered. "You cannot sell us. We're not slaves!"

"He means as hostages," her father said to her. "That would be an excellent thing, poppet."

The man regarded her. "You are slaves. Now. Forever." Then he looked back at his leader and listened.

Next, one of the warriors who had captured them spoke up. Another followed after. Her would-be ravisher strode to the piles of sticks, selected one, and carried it to the bonfire. As he railed in his native tongue, the tip of the stick ignited and a cheer rose up.

The pretty woman followed suit, grabbing a stick and holding it against the evil man's until it, too, burned and smoked.

Another woman joined in, and then a man. And then the little boy who had hit Isabella with a switch. The pretty woman walked up to the tall man and held her torch out to him. She gestured to Isabella and then to the torch. She stood before him with her arm outstretched.

In a gesture of refusal, he crossed his arms over his chest.

The woman stomped her foot. She spoke again, tried to hand him the burning stick again.

Isabella blurted, "Forgive me, sir, I don't speak your tongue. But we meant no harm. Please, please let us go."

The tall man shook his head, his eyes hooded and piercing. "We cannot let you go. You will bring more white skins."

"My father, Dr. Philip Stevens, is a great healer," she said. "His only wish is to stop sickness. We were on our way to Fort William Henry to save the people there from a terrible plague." She took a breath. "Let him go do his duty and I will stay as your hostage."

"Isabella, no!" her father shouted. "Don't even suggest such a thing."

The evil-looking man spoke again. The tall man pursed his lips and crossed his arms over his chest, but he was studying Isabella's face very closely. It seemed to her that he was searching for something.

Then another woman stomped up to Isabella and showed her a rope. She turned and spoke to Oneko, who had been silent, and gestured that she would start tying Isabella to the stake.

Oneko unfolded his arms and said to Wusamequin in their language, "What does she speak of, this white captive?"

"Her father is a shaman," Wusamequin told him. "He was on his way to heal the white skins of a plague. Her heart hurts that so many will die. She's offered to stay as hostage if we'll allow him to heal the sick ones, and then to return to us."

Odina raised her fist. "Are you mad? They'll bring soldiers back and finish the job they started thirteen moons ago."

"Please, what is she saying?" the white woman—Isabella—asked him in her own tongue.

"That you will tell soldiers of us," he replied. His Yangees was clumsy; he hadn't spoken it in a long time. His people no longer counted any Yangee as welcome in their village.

"No." She shook her head. "My father and I swear on our honor never to tell of you. Only let us conclude this mission of mercy."

*Mercy.* He remembered that word. Her people prayed to a god of goodness and mercy, and James Anderson had explained that word to him very carefully.

"Why show mercy to our enemies?" he flung at her. "Never has honor lived among your people. Not one Yangee speaks with a true heart."

Her face hardened. She stood arrow-straight as she retorted, "You have never met *me* before."

"Wusamequin," Oneko said. "Come here. I will confer with you." He hailed Sasious over as well. "My sons, I will talk a moment."

The two younger men obeyed, standing before Oneko as he spread his arms and addressed the People.

"We are no longer the friend of the Yangees," he said. "But the Yangee war chiefs don't know this. We haven't broken our tomahawk and shown it to them. In matters of the past, today's deaths avenged us."

The villagers began to mutter angrily. Oneko cut them off, raising his hand.

"We have made tentative friends with *les Français*. We have not smoked the peace pipe, but selling this war chief to them would make their hearts rest easier with us."

He turned to Sasious, who was glowering at the ground. "Listen, my son Sasious. *Les Français* will pay us well for a Yangee warrior. Since the white skins came, we have need of their wampum. Although wampum is nothing but useless beads, we must have it. The white skins trade with it. They pay for things among themselves with it. They don't pay in food and weapons, as was our custom before the white skins came."

"They pay in firewater," Sasious spat. "They pay in the poisoning of our young men."

Oneko held up a hand. "If we burn the grayhair, it will be the same as burning a deer or a tomahawk. A waste. I've seen in Wusamequin's eyes that his honor has been restored by the deaths of the other Yangee soldiers today. Is that true, medicine man?"

Wusamequin was annoyed with Oneko. First he told him to bury the hatchet with Sasious, and now he was pitting him against the one man whose honor today had been blighted by Wusamequin himself. Sasious certainly needed no reminders that he, Wusamequin, had stopped him from taking advantage of a captive. But he answered, "My honor has been restored."

"What of *our* honor?" Sasious demanded, his

voice rising. He balled a fist and held it over his head. "We have been destroyed as a people by the white skins! Our sources of food have been pillaged! Tribes of People all over this valley are starving, and why? Because of them!" He pointed at *Mahwah* and Stevens, who were speaking to one another. The girl was trying very hard not to cry.

"We are a strong people," Oneko replied. "We will survive until we find a way to turn the tide. And then we will be rid of all of them."

Sasious closed his eyes and shook his head. "That is a dream, Great Sachem. They are here, and here to stay."

"The spirits will help us be rid of them," Oneko insisted. "But not today."

"You're going to spare them, then." Sasious glared at Wusamequin. "This is *your* doing. An evil spirit has entered our medicine man and weakened his heart."

"Sasious," Oneko said sharply. "I am still your sachem. I can still think for myself. And I am not *sparing* them." He looked hard at both men. Sasious was seething. Wusamequin kept his own counsel and remained impassive.

"I'll send scouts to look for a war chief of *les Français*, one who is able to pay us well for the Yangees. Because of the war, there are several such chiefs in these parts. I'll give each scout a belt that will discuss the terms of selling the hostages. All this I will do within one moon's time. If by then I haven't found a suitable buyer, I'll burn them both at the stake." He adjusted his blanket of office and raised his chin. "Does this satisfy you, Sasious?"

The man lowered his head and said, "Better, Sachem, if you burn the father and give the daughter to me."

Clearly intrigued, Oneko cocked his head. "As your wife or your slave?"

Sasious sniffed with contempt. "My slave. Sasious does not marry white skin women."

Oneko took that in, pondering a moment. He looked neither pleased nor displeased. Then he raised a brow as he turned to Wusamequin. "Do you agree to this, my son?"

Wusamequin couldn't bear the prospect of Mahwah's living in Sasious's wigwam. He knew that the violent war chief would beat her, and take cruel advantage of her; soon all that was beautiful would be ground into dust.

He said, "The white skin woman fought bravely today. She was fierce when the women and children counted coup on her."

Oneko chuckled. "She was a badger."

"That means she'll be a good slave," Sasious replied. "She isn't like most of the white skin women, weaker than an infant. She trekked well back to the village."

"She did not run, as the wounded soldiers did," Wusamequin added grimly.

"But we caught them all. There were no survivors," Sasious reminded him. "My warriors achieved that."

Oneko crossed his arms. "Let us leave it at this: I'll

search for *les Français* until the next moon, which is Cold Moon. We'll take that time to seek counsel from the spirits concerning the fate of the white skin woman, and when we have their answer, we'll follow their advice. But we are agreed that the grayhair shall die if we find no one to purchase him."

Sasious said, "Agreed."

Wasumaquin thought of the grief he had felt upon losing his father. Mahwah's spirit would be crushed. But he lowered his head and said, "Agreed." It was not his problem that her father was a Yangee. It was hers.

Oneko gestured to the captives and said, "I'll put them away again in their wigwam."

"They should be fed," Wusamequin observed. "They haven't eaten." At the surprised expressions on the other men's faces, he said, "They will be more highly prized if they are well. They will be well if they are treated well."

"You have a healer's heart," Oneko said. Then he turned to the waiting crowd, which was growing restive.

"People of the River," he began, "I wish to sell these Yangees to *les Français.*"

There was a roar of disapproval—led, Wusamequin noted, by Odina and her plump sister, Keshkecho. He wondered if her anger was for his sake: after all, the Yangees had killed his woman. Here was a chance to exactly even the score, by killing one of theirs.

His heart was troubled. He had no idea why he cared so much about the fate of this enemy. Sasious was wise to doubt him. He doubted himself.

He stood beside Sasious as Oneko led the People down the path of his decision. Sasious was their war leader; Wusamequin was their medicine man—the two men formed a picture of placid solidarity with their sachem. But as his look shifted to Mahwah, his heart was tormented. He wondered if she had bewitched him in some way to make him falter thus.

He needed to confer with Great Bear. His guide would help sort out the way of his heart in this.

He was startled out of his reverie as Oneko said to Sasious, "Choose a strong warrior to guard them."

Mingled among the other villagers, the braves straightened, awaiting the honor of being selected. The captives had been declared valuable property, and standing watch over them would aid the tribe. Hence, doing so would enhance the reputation of whomever was selected.

"Wematin," Sasious said, gesturing to the young man. Wematin swaggered from the circle and approached the burning stakes, where the captives were still secured. He barked orders at two more braves, and the trio began untying Mahwah and Stevens.

The other villagers registered their disapproval with hisses and raised fists. But no one laid a hand on Mahwah or her father as they were escorted from the tribal circle.

Wusamequin stayed as he was, watching with a stone face.

*Her people murdered your family,* he reminded himself.

*She is nothing to you. And it would be an easy thing to give her to Sasious. Oneko said to give him a thing of value.*

*She is nothing to me.*

But as the three muscular braves grouped around her and her father, and she disappeared from his gaze, his heart whispered back, *You are lying.*

Wusamequin participated in the *keutikaw*, the ritual feast to bid farewell to his dead wife and son. He ate squirrel, trout, and moose. He danced and urged his family to take the Road of Stars. Their time in the Land Beyond was done.

The village said good-bye as well, many with long faces. His wife had been well liked. High hope had been placed on his son that he would grow up to be a credit to his grandfather's shamanistic legacy.

Odina was sweet smiles and pretty looks, as if to say that now that his mourning was over, she would entice him into her wigwam.

He turned his back on the circle and began to walk toward the forest. He needed to be alone, to sort out his confusing feelings. His heart was at war with itself.

There was an old riddle among his people: *There are two wolves in your heart. One wolf is fear and one wolf is courage. Both are evenly matched, and both are willing to fight to the death. And yet, one wolf will win. Which wolf will it be?*

*The answer is: the one you feed.*

He frowned, wondering why the riddle had come to mind. If its rising in his thoughts was Great Bear's way of trying to tell him something. If so, he didn't understand the message. There was nothing he feared. He was a warrior.

He walked from the village into the tall stands of chestnuts and sumacs. Overhead, a thousand stars glittered, the monument of the Mother of All, whose body was the earth and all its beauty. He gazed up at them, his face dry of tears, and whispered to his dead wife, "Are you free now?"

He covered his eyes with the knuckles of his hands and breathed in slowly, deliberately breathed out. He leaned back his head and shut tight his lids, allowing the moon to see him. This moon was called Hunter's Moon. The brown leaves stood for the pelts of the game the hunters killed; the yellow leaves stood for the fat. The next moon, the one that would end Mahwah's life no matter what became of her, was called Cold Moon. He would call it the Moon of Dead Spirits, for it would signal the end of hers.

*It is of no matter. She is only a white skin woman.*

He came to a clearing that glowed with moonlight. He reached into his medicine bag and filled his fist with pollen, which he held into the night breeze and allowed to scatter. Then he took his shirt off, exposing his bare chest to the gaze of the night.

He used sign language to say, *I call Great Bear to me again. I have need of his wise counsel again.*

Then he sat cross-legged in the center of the meadow, and waited for his totem to speak. He sat with his back straight and his head up. He was alert.

Then Great Bear formed in the sky above him, the stars dancing and twirling. He heard the voices of his ancestors raised in a chant, saw their finery as they capered and pranced around the great council fire.

*Your time has come, Wusamequin.*
*Wusamequin, We of the Land Beyond decree*
*That your time has come.*

His lids grew heavy; he began to doze, and to dream. He saw Great Bear form in the night mists and moonlit clouds and slowly descend to earth before him. As the ghostly paws settled against the dewy grasses, Wusamequin felt his body melt; his head fell forward on his chest, and then slowly, he lay on his side, the grass sheltering him.

The wind breezed over him, and the night caressed the scar on his back. He saw in his mind his wife walking the trail of the stars, his child bundled in a board on her back.

She stopped once and turned, gazing down on him with such love that in his sleep he moaned, tormented. His heart cried out, *Come back to me. Come back, come back.*

And Great Bear whispered: *Your wolves are not fear and courage, my human nephew. They are grief and hope.*

# ❖ *Chapter Eight* ❖

*I*n the hut, Isabella's Indian jailer yawned. Father and daughter said not a word. Dr. Stevens kept his gaze fixed on the ground, and Isabella followed suit.

They had been given steamed fish and a sort of corn pudding filled with dried blueberries and nuts. Also, water to drink. After they had finished, their hands had been tied behind their backs. Her shoulders ached.

The muscular guard, dressed in leggings, a breechcloth, and a leather shirt, narrowed his eyes as he studied them, his hatred nearly a living thing. At his mocassined feet lay a scalping knife and a tomahawk. Isabella was certain he would have no qualms about using them if they did anything to displease him—and claim later, perhaps, that they had tried to escape. Such were these savages—lying, deceitful, evil.

She had no idea how much time passed; but after a time, the man's lids began to flicker. He roused himself, straightening his shoulders. Then it happened once more.

At the same time, she sensed her father's eyes on her. She turned her head the merest fraction of an inch, and followed his line of sight as he shifted his attention to the back of the hut.

The four walls of the hut were made of tree limbs, covered over with mats that reminded her of thatch. She studied the place that he scrutinized, trying to see what he was trying to show her. In some places, there was a little more space between the sections, and there she could see the dark night sky. But there was nothing truly out of the ordinary, at least to her untrained eye.

Her father looked back at her, then again to the same area in the hut.

She knit her brows and gave her head a shake to show him that she didn't understand what he was trying to tell her.

The guard yawned, drawing the attention of both father and daughter. Isabella tried to watch him without giving the appearance of doing so. He fought a second yawn, but eventually gave in to it; simply observing him made Isabella feel tired.

In the distance, an owl hooted. Isabella thought mournfully of her feather bed back in Albany; and of Fort William Henry. Surely, search parties had been sent out from there to look for them.

The guard shifted, spreading his legs farther apart to help him with his balance. He yawned a third time. Then, as she watched in astonishment, his arms dropped to his sides; his head lolled forward; and he slowly sank to the floor like a character in a fairy story who has been enchanted. He sprawled out on the ground and began to softly snore.

Isabella gaped at him, blinking in surprise. The only people she had ever seen faint dead away were women overcome by what was commonly referred to as "the vapors"—but which she now realized were simply cases of being laced in their corsets too tightly. Something else had put this man to sleep. Was he ill? She thought of the pestilence at the fort. Had it traveled here in some fashion, perhaps through the night air?

After a few seconds, her father began to scoot toward the guard. Without speaking, he urged her to follow his example. Her heart pounded at the thought of moving closer to the man. She found it was easier to walk on her knees, though she was still off-balance and clumsy, tripping herself up on the remnants of her skirt.

Longer-limbed and wearing trousers, which gave greater ease of movement, her father outpaced her; with a quick, grim smile, he worked his way toward the knife and turned to the side, bending backward in a diagonal line in an effort to grab it up. His fingers stretched as his hands hovered just inches from his target. He bent farther back, and this time his fingertips brushed the blade. But he could not seem to manage to pick up the weapon.

He straightened back up on his knees and huffed in quiet frustration. Isabella took a deep breath and crept on her knees up beside him. Then she copied his movements, bending sideways and down . . . and grabbed up the knife.

She caught her breath. Her father gazed at her steadily, and she crept over to him. She turned her back, and she felt him painstakingly easing the knife out of her hand. She remained as she was; soon she felt him sawing through the rope.

Though it cost her in discomfort, she pulled her hands apart as hard as she could. He continued to saw; she continued to pull.

Then her right hand sprang free. She swallowed down her joyful cry and remained still as he sawed at the left hand. Then she yanked her hand hard, and that one was free, too.

Painful tingles shot up and down her hands and arms. She rubbed them together, flexing her fingers, until some ease of movement was restored to them.

Eagerly she pivoted around and took the knife from her father. Her hands still tingling, she sawed through his restraints, not as agile with the blade as he.

*What if someone comes to check on us?* she thought anxiously, glancing toward the flap. The brave was snoring quietly; she would have been surprised if anyone outside the hut could hear him, but perhaps someone would come to relieve him, or bring him some food.

*We must hurry! And be out of here!*

Then it was done; she cut through the final shreds of rope and they dangled from her father's wrists. He grimaced but made no sound as he rubbed his hands for circulation. Then he put his finger to his lips just as Major Whyte had done. For a moment, recalling the man, Isabella was strangled with grief and fear, her mind skimming over all the horrors she had seen in the last day and night.

Then her father grabbed up the tomahawk and arced it over his head, ready to smash it down on the head of the sleeping Indian.

It was the wise thing to do; if their guard awoke and found them missing, he would sound the alarm and they would be captured, and probably punished. Maybe even burned.

But a voice inside Isabella's head whispered, *Do not harm him.*

She shook her head violently, imploring her father with her eyes. He frowned at her, the tomahawk held high over his head.

This time she reached her arms forward to stay his hand, extending them protectively above the Indian's head. Her father huffed angrily; he would not be stopped. She shook her head again and tapped her temple, mouthing, *"Please."*

He signaled that he didn't understand, but when she would not relent, he lowered the tomahawk and wiped his forehead, clearly beyond frustrated with her. He stared at her as if she were mad. She knew she was asking the impossible, but she did so anyway.

Resolutely, she mouthed, *"No."*

He glanced at the entrance flap, then at the tomahawk, as if deciding what to do next. Perhaps he was afraid she would make so much noise with her protests that either the brave would rouse or someone would come.

She gave her head a shake.

She prayed that the look he gave her in return would someday not hurt so much. Then he slowly got to his feet and tiptoed to the rear of the hut. Isabella followed suit.

He carefully lowered himself onto the earthen floor and grabbed a bit of matting stretched perpendicular with the floor. As he gazed meaningfully first at it, and then at her, he pulled on it.

The matting crumbled in his hand. It was rotted clean through.

So that was what he had been trying to tell her! Filled with hope, she wrapped her hands around the next limb, and it disintegrated into moist chunks that stuck to her fingers.

She cleared off another branch, and another, while her father moved the bits away from the crawl space they were making. He glanced often in the direction of the brave. He still held the tomahawk, and Isabella could tell that he still wished to use it on the man.

When she had made a space that would accommodate him, she tugged at his sleeve. They smiled grimly at each other. This was the moment of truth. He got down on his knees and held himself up with one hand and he peered out of the space. They both sat back on their heels and exchanged silent prayers. Her only parent; his only child.

Then he pointed at her. He was telling her to go first. When she began to refuse, he pointed at the brave. She understood: Her refusal to let him kill their guard was the reason he wanted her to get out ahead of him. And she also understood that he would not bend, as she had not.

She took a deep breath. She was afraid, but she must do this.

She pointed to herself again, and then to the space, thinking, *It would be nice if we could speak to each other with our hands, as the savages do.* And then she had the fleeting thought, *Perhaps they are not so uncivilized after all, if they can manage such a thing.*

Her father looked down at the tomahawk and the knife, as if deciding between the two. Then he handed her the knife. His eyes welled with tears, and she leaned forward and brushed her lips with his. With his good arm, he pulled her against his chest and held her tightly, whispering, "God bless you, Isabella."

The brave snorted and smacked his lips. They jerked apart and glanced at him, Isabella's grip tightening around the knife. He slept on.

Quickly, Isabella put the knife between her teeth, as she had done before, turned over on her back, and began to slide through the hole. It was more than sufficient for her; they had sized it to fit her father, and he was a robust man.

Her head poked free and she gazed up at stars and treetops. She looked left and right, and saw no one.

She scrambled out, and knelt to help her father. Despite his injury, he was able to slither out like a snake.

Now they were out of the hut; it seemed another miracle that no one else was about. They said nothing, but crept through the village as silently as they knew how. They passed a hut shaped as theirs had been; then another, much longer and taller.

The trees grew denser. They were entering the woods, pitch black with the night. She wondered what had become of their horses, and wished desperately that they could find one and ride off so fast that no one could follow.

But that was not to be. And although she was exhausted, she did her best to match her father's pace as he gripped her by the upper arm and hurried her along. She had no idea how she managed it; her feet were nearly floating above the ground, she was so light-headed and faint.

"If we are separated, keep going," he whispered to her. "Under no circumstances are you to look for me or to double back." He pointed at the sky. "See that bright star? Look for it. Follow it. Find the path where we were attacked and follow it. If Indians come, hide. If soldiers come, look for their officers and present yourself to them."

"Yes, Papa," she murmured anxiously. She hefted the knife in her left hand. She cleared her throat and said, "In this case, Papa, might it not be . . . permissible . . . for a young Christian woman to take her own life, rather than fall into the hands of savages?"

Her father faltered as he walked. "Oh, my dear girl," he moaned. "I should have left you in Albany. I curse myself for my selfishness. Cora said I should have left you."

"No, Papa," she said softly. "For in that case, you would surely be dead by now."

She wasn't certain if he heard her. They stumbled on, holding on to one another.

And then she heard the distant yipping of a wolf. She scanned the dark woods, unable to see anything,

Then she realized that it was coming from behind them. It had to be the tame wolf she had seen in the village.

"We've been discovered!" her father whispered.

His grip on her tightened as he broke into a run. The trees rushed up; a branch smacked her in the face. Then another.

Then her father's grip broke loose, and she was running forward madly in the darkness, flailing for him.

"Papa? Papa?" she whispered fiercely.

The wolf's yip was growing louder, and louder still. She ran left, right, the dense growth catching her clothes and tossing her about, almost as if the trees themselves were trying to catch her. Then the ground abruptly dipped, and she was unprepared; she stumbled forward, unable to see where she was going.

An agonizing stab of heat shot through her left thigh. The pain exploded throughout her body, all of a piece. She fell forward, smacking her head on a tree trunk. She had run directly into a broken branch that had pierced her leg. Her shaking hand found it, sticking straight out of her thigh; blood was gushing freely around it, coating both her hands.

"No," she managed, and then the pain and the shock were too great.

As she fell backward, the branch ripped a few inches upward, enlarging the wound. She barely felt it; she was sinking into a dead faint.

The wolf howled eagerly, and the dogs bayed with bloodthirsty joy.

*They will find me. And if I am not dead by then, they will surely kill me.*

The barking dogs called Wusamequin. He jerked up from his damp bed of grass and hastily got to his feet. Senses sharp, he cocked his head and listened. Afraid-of-Everything was with the pack. Something was on the run.

Not far from where he stood, something rustled in a patch of wild blackberry bushes. He pulled out his knife and darted toward it. As he lunged forward into the growth, the moon gleamed over his shoulder and bathed the still form of Mahwah, lying on her side.

He dropped to his knee and touched her shoulder. She did not move. Then he trailed his hand from her arm down her side to her thigh. Blood was gushing from a deep wound in her leg. Alarmed, he put his hand over it, pressing down hard; but it was a useless gesture. The blood was pooling around her body as if she were lying in a stream.

With his knife he slit open one of his leggings, creating a long strip of leather. He slammed it down over the wound and quickly tied it around her leg. Then he reached into his medicine bag and brought out his medicine bundle, which he pressed against her wound.

"*Oh, Great Spirit, Pachtamawas, let her soul stay among us for a time,*" he chanted.

The wolf and the dogs bounded up, Afraid-of-Everything delighting in the discovery that his master was there. He nosed Wusamequin for a treat, but the shaman ignored him. Afraid-of-Everything whined and sat back on his haunches, cocking his head.

Wusamequin slid his hands beneath Mahwah and lifted her in his arms. He wondered where her father was. Dead, caught trying to escape?

*We should have realized that this one could not be held down,* he thought, surveying her slack features. *That she is a warrior among her people, in her own way.* And yet so delicate, almost fawnlike. She reminded him of his dead wife, who had also been fragile, but stronger than a birch tree.

He was sorry to take her back to the village, but he had no other choice. Her wound was grievous. If he was to save her life, he had to get to his more elaborate medicines as quickly as possible. As it was, she had already lost so much blood that he wasn't certain he could bring her back from her path to the Land Beyond.

He was surprised by how much that bothered him.

By the time he reached the village, most of the People were up and out of their wigwams. Oneko greeted him, frowning down at the woman. Sasious stood beside him, scarlet with fury.

"One accounted for," the sachem said angrily. "But not the prize."

Sasious scowled at Mahwah and hissed, "I'd like to scalp her right now." He grunted. "By the looks of all that blood, she'll be dead soon anyway."

"We cannot let her die," Wusamequin said quickly.

"We should have killed them when we had the chance," Sasious countered.

Oneko raised a hand. "Wusamequin speaks rightly. It appears that the father has escaped."

Sasious said, "The braves will find him and hunt him down. He won't see another sunrise."

"I hope that you're right, my son," Oneko told him. "But until we do, we must keep this one alive. The only weapon we have against him is his daughter, as our living hostage. As long as we have her, he may fear to make war upon us." He nodded at the medicine man. "Do all you can for her."

The sachem turned and faced the People. "We must move," he announced. "Until dawn we will prepare. And then we must go. If he escapes, the Yangee officer will return with soldiers. Wusamequin will ask the spirits where we should go. It will be a new place, one the Yangees have never heard about from us."

In the moonlight, alarm and worry creased the faces of the People. He surveyed the throng facing him; most of the braves had already left. He assumed they were scouring the forest for Stevens.

"She's more valuable than ever," Wusamequin said. "I'll take her to your wigwam, Oneko." Her protection would be greatest there. No one would dare harm a possession of the tribal leader.

"No." Wabun-Anung, Oneko's wife, stepped forward. She glowered first at Mahwah, and then at him. "I will not have that pale skin witch in my home. She bewitched Wematin and made him fall asleep." She sniffed. "Only the medicine man should be expected to deal with such a person."

Wusamequin hesitated, sensing that he stood on swampy ground. He doubted she had bewitched Wematin, but it would help the young warrior save face to say she had. He would not add to the young man's humiliation.

"It was either the white skin woman, or someone else," Sasious declared. "Perhaps someone whose heart was too weak to burn her."

Wusamequin held his council, but inwardly, he seethed at the accusation. He didn't have time to wage war with Sasious. But he would not forget this slight.

He raised his chin and said, "If Wabun-Anung is unhappy with the hostage in her wigwam, then I'll take her to mine."

"Yes, take 'Mahwah,'" Odina hissed angrily. Her face was taut with hurt, and Wusamequin was sorry.

He looked straight at her and said, "Oneko has declared that she must live. If I'm to fulfill his request, I must care for her immediately."

"Yes. Go," Oneko urged him. Then he swept his arm toward Sasious and Odina and added, "There are words between many of the words that have been spoken here. We'll discuss those later."

Wusamequin moved through the crowd, heading for his wigwam. There were hostile mutterings; he ignored them. His heart was pounding and sweat beaded his brow.

*I must save her,* he thought. *She is very valuable.*

The spirits of the wind whispered, "*To whom, Wusamequin? She is valuable to whom?*"

And joining the airy words, Great Bear growled gently inside his heart, as if to say, *Keep walking your path, my human nephew. Your feet are finding their way.*

# ❧ Chapter Nine ❧

*C*hanting?

Isabella heard rattling and smelled smoke. The room floated and swirled; she felt as if she were floating up through the stars. Then she began walking on stars, in a vast meadow of stars. Stars hung from the trees; a zephyr breeze scattered tiny stars no bigger than a diamond.

Someone walked beside her, holding her hand. The hand was strong and powerful; and it was a reddish copper against her white skin. The veins on the back of the hand were pronounced; the wrist was thick with muscle.

"Your heart is heavy with sorrow," said a deep, masculine voice. "It may not live through the night."

Her head tilted back to see a tall, handsome man. She knew him, but she could not remember why. Stars glittered at the corners of his eyes; she lifted a hand and touched one. It was a tear. He was crying.

"My heart is wounded as well," he said to her. "We are both sick in our spirits."

The stars blurred and shimmered; he moved away from her and began to chant in his native tongue, the nonsensical words of a savage. He was half-naked, wearing only a loincloth, and there were symbols inscribed on his chest. He was holding two palm-size spheres across which leather had been stretched, and he was shaking them in rhythm to his chant.

Isabella dozed, and dreamed she was in Albany again, with Mrs. DeWitt. The apple-cheeked woman was wearing burgundy and gold, and wearing a mob-cap from which wisps of gray hair poked. She sat across from Isabella in the damask sitting room of the DeWitt home in Albany. They were having tea; and the dear woman leaned forward, pushing Isabella's hair away from her face and said, "My poor little darling, you're burning up with fever."

The scene dissolved before her eyes as Isabella flushed from the crown of her head to her heels with unbearable heat. She became dimly aware that she had on no clothes, and that something was heaped over her body, making her very, very hot.

Weakly she batted at the burdensome weight. Then she heard the sound of rattles and a man chanting in a deep, low voice.

She felt a wet, cool cloth on her forehead; with great care and tenderness, the cloth moved from across her brow down the right side of her face, and then her left. She whimpered. She hurt, and her leg felt as if some-one had dropped burning embers into the center of it.

She mumbled, "Papa?"

The cloth was taken away, and came back even cooler. Then something was placed beneath her nose. She smelled a wonderful scent, something flowery and spicy at the same time, and she gladly inhaled it. Fainter, the ruddy scent of smoke wafted toward her, as if someone were fanning a fire.

The chanting began again. She tried to speak, but her mouth was too tired. She tried to move to push away the mound on top of her, but she couldn't move so much as a finger.

Then her father was leaning over her; there were his kind brown eyes, his salt-and-pepper brows knit with worry. He held her hand, stroked her forehead, and whispered, "You are very ill, Mahwah. You must help me chase the evil spirits from your body and your spirit."

"Yes." That was reasonable.

She heard more singing. She was confused; could it be Papa? He only sang in church. The pitch varied, from low to high and back again, carrying her along with it until she felt as if it were a wave on the ocean, and she rode a storm-tossed boat. She stood at the rail with her mother's arm around her; she wore her pale green traveling coat, gloves, and a hat. The wind lufted the sails; the seamen scrambled as the officers called out orders beneath a lowering sky.

Her mother put her arm around Isabella and smiled lovingly at her. She said, "Stay with me, my little Bella. Don't go ashore. I've missed you so."

Her father continued to sing as Isabella put both her arms around her mother's neck and pressed her face into the lace fichu scented with perfume. Her mother, her mother. Her heart pounded with happiness.

"Yes, Mama, I shall," she told her. "I shall stay."

Then a different man's voice murmured, "Mahwah. Fight. The demons come to trick you."

She recognized that voice. Perspiration trickled down her forehead as she panicked. Where was she? What had happened to her mother and father?

Then she stood on the deck of the ship with her mother once more. Emily Stevens's perfume enveloped her; the sea smelled clean and new and fresh. "My Bella," her mother murmured, cradling her head. "Stay with me always, my sweet."

"Mama." She held her more tightly, sinking against her. All her terrors faded. "I had such a terrible dream," she said. We were captured by savages." She gripped her hard. "But you . . . you were dead by then. In my . . . dream."

She began to sob. "Thank God it wasn't true." Tears rolled down her cheeks. "It wasn't true!"

"Mahwah, I will fight with you," a man whispered.

"No, no," she moaned, clinging to her mother. "No! Mama!"

Then she opened her eyes, and screamed.

A monster perched on her chest. It sat back on its haunches like a cat. Its face was black and blue; its eyes were slitted and glowed like embers. Its ears fanned upward like a bat's.

It smiled at her, huge teeth glistened; then its fanged jaws opened wide as it leaned forward, as if to engulf her entire head.

A man loomed above the creature, holding a war

club. He wore only a breechcloth; his muscular chest, legs, and feet were bare. His face was painted. His face was blue and dotted with black. He whirled in a circle, holding the club to his chest; as he rotated around, he extended his arms. The club swiped at the monster, but the creature ducked, leaping off Isabella's chest and hurtling itself at the man.

It slammed into his chest, knocking the man backward. The man hit the earthen floor hard, then rolled to the left, taking the creature with him. The monster lay beneath him. The man rose up on his knees, arced his war club over his head, and brought it down on the creature's face.

It bellowed and screamed, slashing at him. One of the talons sliced his cheek; his response was to pummel it a second time with his club.

The creature shrieked with rage. The man leaped to his feet, straddling the monster. He leaned forward and gripped the monster by its shoulders, grunting as he forced it to a standing position. As it wobbled, he threw down his club and began to chant. He made fists and threw himself at the monster, head-butting it in the abdomen.

The creature staggered backward. Then the man began to dance. He extended his arms to the side and stamped his feet against the ground, whirling in a circle. His hair whipped like a cape around his face. His back and chest glistened with sweat. He lifted one knee and whirled in another circle, his voice rising and falling, cresting and waving . . .

Isabella stood on the deck of the ship again; her mother slowly released her, gazing sadly at her. She said, "Now is not our time, my Bella. Our time has passed."

Fog rolled across the deck as her mother stepped away from her, slowly waving. The fog thickened; her mother glided backward into it, touching her fingers to her lips and blowing Isabella a kiss . . .

"Mama!" she screamed, throwing open her arms. "No!"

Then the man spun in a circle around the monster, stamping his feet harder, harder; his voice was insistent—*hey-a, hey-a!* The monster lunged at him, its talons flashing. But its movements were duller. Its roar, softer.

He danced; and as she watched, he attacked the monster again, kicking and punching it; blood gushed from its fanged mouth. It batted at him.

Then he pulled a knife from his breechcloth and drove it straight into the monster's heart.

The thing threw back its enormous head and screamed, and he picked it up and hurled it against a wall made of thatch.

It shattered into pieces, and each piece became a shooting star.

Isabella stared mutely, too stunned to make a sound. Her forehead trickled with sweat and she was suddenly quite cold.

Then she fainted dead away.

✢✢ ✢✢ ✢✢

"Mahwah."

Isabella started. Her eyes flew open to find the tall man standing over her. Then, as she took in the wall of matting behind him, the horrible realization hit her: She was back in the prison hut.

She broke down. "We didn't make it," she sobbed. "Oh, please, please, what have you done to my father?"

A hand slipped beneath her heavy coverlet and wrapped around her bare shoulder. It held tight as she surrendered to all the fear and horror of the last days, weeping miserably, completely at a loss. She had never felt so defeated and hopeless in her entire life.

She was so sick and exhausted that she stopped sobbing almost as soon as she had begun. Then she lay passively, her eyes half-closed, as tears streamed down her blank face. She felt her mind leaving, as if it could no longer bear the weight of everything that had happened to her.

"Your father lives," the man said gently, steadily. "Mahwah, your father lives."

"Wh . . . what?" she asked, holding her breath. She tried to turn over to look at him, but the weight upon her was too heavy. She realized that a heap of furs had been lain over her. She wondered if her fevered mind had turned them into a demon; she vaguely remembered dreams, good and bad. She understood that she had been delirious. No matter; a thousand demons could plague her if only her father were alive.

He released her, and walked around her head to

face her on her other side, apparently so that she could see him comfortably without moving. She ticked her glance up to him, and caught her breath. She had never seen a man in so few clothes as he, and it seemed unbearably intimate to look him in the eye.

She said to him, "Where is my father?"

He replied, "Stevens ran into the forest."

*He escaped*, she realized, her heart flooding with happiness. *He made it. I . . . I did not. But he'll come for me.*

The man crossed his ankles, then sank easily down beside her. She swallowed hard. "I ran into a tree branch," she said.

He nodded, settling his forearms on his knees. His unearthly paint gave him the aspect of a demon. Dim images of a battle between him and a terrifying creature flashed in her mind, but she couldn't quite recall them. Still, it made her feel even shyer around him, thinking of how bravely he had fought . . . and on her account. Rather like a knight doing battle for his lady, instead of a half-naked savage overheating her with tanned animal hides.

"What is to become of me?" she asked him.

He cocked his head and did not answer. She didn't know if he didn't understand, or if he didn't know.

Or if he didn't want to say.

He reached to the left, where he picked up a clay bowl, examining the contents as he swirled it. Satisfied, he gazed at her and made a show of taking a drink, as if to assure her that it was safe. Swallowing, he set down the bowl. Raising up, he slipped his arm under her shoulders, and helped her sit up just enough to sip from the bowl.

Accustomed to the foul taste of medicine, she braced herself as he put the bowl to her lips. But to her surprise, the liquid was rather sweet. She looked at him questioningly, and he said, "*Menachk*. Drink more."

She obeyed, feeling somewhat refreshed. He studied her face, gazing at her eyes, and lay her back down. Then he slipped his hands beneath the heavy pile of furs. His fingertips grazed her thigh; her leg jerked with pain.

She gasped, "Please, don't touch it."

He clenched his jaw; a muscle jumped in his cheek as he took one of his hands from beneath the furs, grabbed up something, and moved his hand back toward the wound.

The pain was unbelievable. Unimaginable.

She screamed and screamed and screamed and—

—She awoke to discover that she was lying on a portable bed of sorts, which was being dragged behind an animal that she could not see. She was dressed in native garb, which was surprisingly soft and supple to the touch. There were colorful quill designs on the bodice, and the sleeves were fringed. She touched her hair, to discover that it had been plaited into two long braids. A headband held them in place.

*Who dressed me?* she wondered shyly. No man had so much as seen her in her chemise since she was an infant.

She let go of that disturbing thought, delighted to

see that she was in the forest again. The trees shimmered in their autumn garb and birds and squirrels capered away as Indians walked all around her. Dressed warmly in leather clothes, the women carried large bundles wrapped in furs or leather. An elderly squaw shuffled to the far left, balancing a pot on her head. Babies jostled along on cradleboards. Men were weighed down with weapons: tomahawks, spears, and bows and arrows.

In his leather jerkin, his hair pulled up and secured by a silver clasp, a silver earring dangling from his right earlobe and wearing a choker of colorful beads, the man strode beside her bed with his tame wolf beside him. The wolf seemed to notice her first; then he made a chuffing sound that alerted his master.

The man looked down at the wolf, and then at Isabella. His features softened as he said, "*Aquai.*" He looked at her. "*Aquai,* Mahwah."

"*Aquai.*" The world felt strange on her lips.

"Wusamequin," he replied. His face was strangely light, his mouth almost curved into a smile as he touched his chest. "Wusamequin."

"That is your name," she realized. He nodded. "Ah! And I . . . well, you know that I am Isabella."

"You are called in the manner of Mahwah," he corrected.

She swallowed. "As you wish." *For now. But I will never, ever forget that I am Isabella Anne Stevens, and an Englishwoman.*

"What is happening?" she asked, looking around. "Where are we going?"

"The People of the River travel," he told her. "A new village. The Yangees will not find us."

"Oh." Her stomach clutched. *Then how will Papa ever find me?*

He looked at her with his dark, deep-set eyes and said, "If the Yangees come, Mahwah stands between us and them. Our hostage."

She swallowed. "Oh. So I'm . . . I'm not going to the French, then?"

He regarded her steadily. "No."

Her emotions confused her. On the one hand, she was more likely to be treated in a civilized manner by the French. They might even return her to her father in a gesture of gallantry—French officers were civilized men, for all of their being warmongers.

But part of her was vastly relieved that she would not be sent away from Wusamequin. That alarmed her. *It's because he nursed me, and has looked after me,* she assured herself. *I may not have such a good friend among the French.*

"Your wound was deep," he continued. "You lost much. . . ." He thought for a moment. "Your spirit came out of you."

*Blood loss,* she translated in her mind. She was a trifle amused at his naive way of putting it. He was a healer, true, but he was also a superstitious native who had never been to a proper medical college.

"It was very kind of you to care for me," she answered, inclining her head.

"To save your life," he countered. He looked hard at her. "Mahwah, you and Stevens ran. You, Mahwah, traveled to the Land Beyond."

She frowned. "I . . . the what?"

"The Land Beyond." He closed his eyes as if to illustrate. There was something deeply eerie in his face—the cast of his skin, the absolute slackness of his muscles. He looked like a corpse.

*I nearly died,* she translated, a chill rushing up her spine. "You would have run too, sir, would you not?" she asked.

His stern expression softened. "I would run."

"But I haven't been punished," she asked, not wanting to ask, but needing to know. In England, sometimes prisoners who were injured were made well before their punishments were meted out. When he didn't appear to understand, she said, "My father and I ran. I came back. But I was not . . . hurt more."

He nodded and looked at her earnestly. "You did not kill Wematin. That spoke to the heart of Oneko. He said not to hurt you more."

*I knew it!* she thought, relief flooding through her. *I knew we oughtn't kill our guard.*

He raised a cautioning hand. "Oneko saw your spirit. But there are others who see a Yangee woman, and death lives in their hearts. Walk with care, Mahwah."

"When I *can* walk." She shifted her legs, and found

to her surprise that her thigh was no longer throbbing with pain. He smiled and raised his chin in an expression of pride that reminded her of her father. But his face was darker and the angles and planes were much sharper. Her father had a gentle English face. She wondered if she would ever see that beloved face again.

"You healed me," she said to him. "Thank you."

"*Wneeweh*," he replied. "Thank you in our tongue."

She licked her lips. "*Wneeweh*."

"*Wunneet*. It is good." He gestured to her bed. "Sleep, Mahwah. Your spirit has fought bravely. It must sleep now."

"When will we be at the new village?" she asked.

He shrugged. "Oneko, Sasious, and Wusamequin—I—will say." He held up three fingers.

So it was to be a joint decision among Wusamequin, who was her personal physician; Oneko, the head of the tribe, who had decreed that she go unpunished for trying to escape; and Sasious, the man who had tried to burn her at the stake. They were the three leaders. The thought that Sasious might hold her fate in his hands disturbed her greatly.

The thought that she might never see her father again shattered her.

*Perhaps it would be better to go to the French*, she thought.

But she had no say in the matter. It appeared that she had no say in anything.

She was pondering that, when the pretty woman

who had taken her earbob sidled up to Wusamequin. Her black hair was pulled up and threaded down her back in a single braid. She was carrying a cumbersome bundle, and Isabella noted that Wusamequin made no offer to take it from her, although he was walking barehanded.

The woman scrunched up her nose as she looked over at Isabella. Though she was seething, Isabella lowered her gaze. She knew this woman was one of the ones whose hearts wished her dead.

"Mahwah, the manner she is called is Odina," Wusamequin said. The woman raised her chin and narrowed her eyes with disdain, just like a British noblewoman whose presence had been contaminated by a peasant.

Now Isabella had a name to go with the poisonous look. Mindful of Wusamequin's warning, she took a deep breath. "*Wunneet.*"

Odina rolled her eyes and snickered. She spoke to Wusamequin, an imperious little smile on her face, and sauntered away. He looked after her, then back to Isabella.

She said in English, "Death-hearted woman."

One side of his mouth turned up in a lazy grin and he chuckled. The sight warmed her, though she wasn't certain why. She gave him a grin back.

It was a wonderful moment. It was a moment that calmed her, and gave her hope.

Then he raised his hand, gesturing at her bed. "*Travois,*" he said. "*Les Français.* And your *cheval.*"

Her eyes widened. She spoke some French. *Cheval* was the word for horse.

She tried to lift herself up so that she could see beyond the upper lip of the *travois*. Wusamequin reached over and put his hands under her shoulders, then easily raised her into the air. Sure enough, her mare pulled the *travois*. So they had found their horses—or at least Isabella's. The sight of the mare gave her more hope.

She began to scheme. *If I can figure out a way to get to her . . .*

As if he could read her thoughts, Wusamequin frowned at her. "Mahwah, do not run," he said. "Sasious will catch you."

The most dangerous of her enemies. The mere mention of his name set her on edge. She fidgeted with the fur, teasing the bristles with her fingertips as she said, "Wusamequin, I am a Yangee. Why are you so kind to me?"

Her question was met by silence. When she dared to look up at him, a shadow had slipped over his face, concealing him from view.

She waited. At length, he said quietly, "I do not know."

The tribe wound its way deep into the forest, down a ravine, and then up and over a mountaintop. There, Wusamequin burned tobacco and chanted, holding something powdery and yellow in his fist at the four directions of the compass, and then straight up and straight down. Isabella felt a thrill of pride she did not understand as she watched him. She lay no claim to him; his actions had nothing to do with her.

The mountains were lavender; the valleys green, lush, and untamed. The transcendent natural beauty surrounded and enfolded both her and the savages who held her captive. Surely God would be merciful, and no harm would come to her. She could not imagine that cruelty could exist alongside such harmony; that a day of mustard-colored sunshine could bring anything but happiness.

*Have a care, Isabella*, she told herself. *You know much of tragedy. You know that fate can tiptoe in and take away all your reason for joy.*

The day had been long; as dusk fell, Wusamequin still walked beside her *travois*. He had remained at her side nearly all day, and several times carried her into the forest so that she could relieve herself. He had given her dried meat and more of their tasty bread dotted with nuts and dried berries. When she was finished, he urged her to drink her fill of berry juice. Then he gave her more dried meat to feed his tame wolf, whose name he translated for her as Afraid-of-Everything.

"It's a strange name," she said to him as the yellow-eyed wolf gazed at her. "He doesn't seem particularly fearful." In case she spoke in overly complicated language, she added, "He is not afraid of everything."

"He was called in the manner of Afraid-of-Everything as a baby." He reached down and affectionately scratched the wolf behind his ears, his face relaxing into a smile.

Then the smile faded as quickly as it had appeared. "His mother was killed. My wife . . ." He clamped his mouth shut, a cloud passing over his face. He seemed angry, but she couldn't be certain. He was impossible to read.

"He is my son now," he said finally. Then he spoke to the wolf in his language. The animal listened, and chuffed as if in answer. Wusamequin said, "He will guard you."

After that, the creature would not leave her side, not even when Wusamequin was called away by the chief to discuss their route. And Isabella realized she had another guard. In this place where she was a hostage, could she have a real friend?

She twisted around and watched Wusamequin standing ahead and to one side of the column of Indians, deep in conversation with Sasious and Oneko. She knew they were assessing their route, trying to devise the surest path to keep the British off their trail.

*Will I ever see my father again?* she wondered.

The yellow-eyed wolf gazed at her with his head cocked as if to say, *I do not know.*

# ❖ Chapter Ten ❖

𝒯he sky was nearly dark by the time the People stopped moving for the night. The misty heather mountains blurred to purple, and then to gray. The vibrant colors of autumn leeched to dark yellow, then gray as well.

Wusamequin had taken his leave of her while she'd been asleep. Afraid-of-Everything walked stalwartly beside her, then sat back on his haunches as an Indian man she had not seen before put his hand on Dulcie's forelock and the horse halted. Then the man walked away without so much as looking at her.

It was time to make camp, and the natives set to work. Isabella was surprised by how efficiently the untamed wilderness was transformed into a village. Women built several fire rings and brought out cooking pots. Soon the fragrant odors of meat and vegetables wafted through the encampment.

Men created makeshift shelters of branches draped with hides, the weight causing the branches to bend so that small, round, tentlike structures were created. It was quite ingenious, and Isabella thought His Majesty's regiments could benefit from using such an arrangement for the troops. As it now stood, soldiers slept in their bedrolls out in the open; only officers bivouacked tents.

As the villagers gathered around the campfires, Isabella's stomach rumbled. She was very hungry, but she was uncertain what to do. She had no idea if she would be welcome at anyone's fire.

Then Wusamequin appeared with a bowl steaming with savory odors, which he set on a nearby flat-topped boulder. He peeled the furs off her, then slid one hand under her knees and another around her back. He had lifted her in that way all day, to carry her into the bushes for her private duties. But this time he hesitated, shook his head, and moved the one hand from behind her knees to wrap it instead across her chest. Then he hoisted her to a half-standing position and lifted her against his chest.

"You must use your leg," he said.

She remembered how he had held her after the massacre, and felt a sharp panic. Then it subsided, and he carried her to the boulder. He smelled of leather and sweat, but it was not unpleasant. His body was warm. Her face was lodged beneath his jaw line, and the pulse in his throat played against her temple.

She was wearing a leather Indian dress, and below that, leggings. The dress was decorated with dyed quills, which fanned over the bodice in an elaborate spray of wildflowers. His gaze swept over the dress as he handed her the bowl; the sight of a thick, brown stew made her mouth water. Tentatively she dipped her fingers into it, wincing slightly at how hot it was.

As she began to eat, Wusamequin lifted up the hem of her dress, revealing her thigh, which was wrapped in leaves and bound with leather. She was embarrassed, but understood that she must allow him to examine it. She concentrated on her food, so impatient for it that she burned her fingertips. She didn't care.

She leaned over to look at the wound, but the shaman spread his fingers over her thigh and said, "Mahwah, do not look."

"Is it that bad?" she asked anxiously, but he didn't appear to understand her question.

He said, "*Gemeze*. Eat."

Rays of crimson sun hit his cheeks, making them appear rosy. The silver earbob he wore sparkled. His profile was rather . . . noble, actually. He had a very straight nose, and a long neck, for a man. All that hair . . . British men dressed theirs, and the upper classes wore wigs. She tried to imagine him in the clothes of a nobleman—for such he was, within his tribe—and stifled a giggle.

He raised a questioning brow, then dropped his gaze to her thigh. She tried to obey him by continuing to eat her stew. His fingers probed the location of her injury; the tender flesh stung where he touched it. Then a searing pain made her wince and grab his shoulder. He pushed directly on the wound; a pressure built; it hurt worse. Without thinking, she gave his shoulder a smack and cried, "Stop it!"

His lips parted; he looked terribly shocked. Flustered, she glanced down—and saw the hideous, gaping hole in her leg. He had stuffed it full of something green, and pus was oozing out of it.

She screamed.

He clamped his hand over her mouth and jerked her hard. His face inches from hers, he hissed, "Do not cry out."

Above his fingers she stared wide-eyed. His gaze moved from her to their surroundings; she saw heads turned in her direction, stony faces, disapproving expressions.

*They are on the run,* she realized, *from my people.*

Rising from a campfire approximately twenty feet away, Sasious stomped over and began gesticulating at her, speaking rapidly and harshly in his language. He folded his arms across his chest and glowered at her, tilting his head at Wusamequin, who began to speak.

Without breaking eye contact with the brave, he said to her, "Sasious says that if you cry out again, he cuts out your tongue. He says that Oneko permits it. I agree."

She was so shocked that she nearly dropped her bowl of stew. Wusamequin noticed and deftly slid his hand under the bowl, dipping two of his fingers into the contents as if he were merely taking his turn at their communal meal. He continued, "Your people search for you. We run."

"It *hurt*," she murmured, embarrassed. "That's why I cried out."

He shrugged. "A woman of the People does not cry out."

Her eyes filled with tears. "I'm not a woman of the People. I'm an Englishwoman."

"I do not forget, Mahwah," he replied, his voice flat. He turned to Sasious and spoke to him. To Isabella, he said, "Sasious has my truth that you will not cry out."

His truth was his promise, she translated. Flushing, she inclined her head to show her concession. "He has my truth, as well." She raised her chin and ordered herself to look Sasious straight in the eye. "*Wunneet,*" she said firmly.

If she had expected to surprise or shock him, she was disappointed. He blinked, then said something to Wusamequin in their language; he finished off by tapping the tip of his tongue, then turned and walked away.

Both the medicine man and Isabella watched him go. "What did he say?" she asked him.

"Your heart knows," he replied. He handed her back the bowl and showed her some fresh green material. It was dried moss, she now realized.

He took her hand and clamped it onto his shoulder. Gazing at her, he pointed to his nose and said, "Do not cry out."

His hands returned to her thigh. She seized as he started doing things to it. He reached up and pointed to his nose again. She stared at it, her nostrils flaring. He made a show of breathing in slowly;

and just as slowly, exhaling. She understood, and copied his movements.

The pain hovered beyond her endurance. She stared at his nose, and breathed.

Then he was finished. He lowered her dress and handed her back her bowl. He said, "*Wunneet.*"

"*Wneeweh,*" she rasped.

He smiled, pleased, and walked away. She was feeling faint, but she said nothing as she stared at his retreating back.

He went to the nearest campfire and secured another bowl of food. He sat with the others, eating and chatting, ignoring her. Her eyes watered from the effort of sitting upright, and the throbbing pain in her leg. She screwed up her courage and examined the wound. He had repacked it with fresh moss. She saw now that he had also previously sewn it shut, with small stitches such as her father would have used. He appeared to have used some kind of gut. The stitches were still in place; he had not disturbed them as he had cleaned and redressed the wound. He was quite skilled, quite deft.

*Particularly when one takes into account that he is a savage.*

Feeling vulnerable to the stares of everyone, she ate more stew. She had nearly licked the bowl clean when Wusamequin returned. A shy young Indian maiden was with him again; she took Isabella's bowl and vanished into the darkening landscape.

"Mahwah, you sleep with Wusamequin," he announced. Before she could respond, he picked her up in his arms and carried her toward one of the tents. Her thigh hurt; he sniffed, and she remembered to look at his nose.

They moved into some underbrush to a tent beneath a trio of fragrant pines. The young maiden was there, holding open the flap. She lowered her gaze as the spirit warrior carried the English hostage inside.

Inside, bent over because the tent ceiling was low, Wusamequin paused in the dark and murmured, *"Wanakusak."*

A trio of tiny glowing lights appeared at the top of leather hangings, casting soft, muted light on their surroundings. At Wusamequin's feet, a bed of grass had been arranged, a folded fur covering to the right of it. It looked rather narrow for two people, and panic washed over her. Surely he didn't mean to . . . to do anything. He knew she was injured. And her father would see him hung if he realized anything had gone . . . awry.

Wusamequin said, *"Komeekha."*

Then he lay her down on the bed. Her heart was thundering; it skipped a beat as he reached down to the hem of his leather jerkin and pulled it over his head. Bare-chested, he lay beside her on the grass. He unfolded the heavy fur and drew it over both of them.

She couldn't breathe as she braced herself for whatever came next. But he gazed at her for perhaps ten seconds, then rolled over, away from her, and settled in.

He was going to do nothing, leave her in peace. She was grateful to her soul.

She licked her lips and whispered, "*Wneeweh*."

If he heard her, he gave no sign of it.

If she dreamed, she did not remember it.

Dawn crept into the tent, damp and chilly. There was frost on the leather drapes of the tent, and she snuggled more deeply into the fur. Doves cooed; branches rustled. She opened her eyes and listened intently. She assumed that Wusamequin had brought her into his tent to guard her from those who would wish her harm. She sincerely doubted he believed her capable of running. Her injury was too severe.

Wusamequin still slept, his back to her. She stared at his dark hair, seeing that it was not all black. There were rich strands of mahogany, and some closer to dark blue. Seeing his hair tangled and sleep-tossed, she felt a rush of tenderness that she didn't understand, and so she pushed it away.

She had to relieve herself, and had no idea how to manage it without disturbing him. She didn't think that her leg would support her, and she wasn't sure she could force herself to stand on it.

As she pondered what to do, he turned over. His eyes were closed; his face was very close to hers, and his sigh warmed her cheek. His breath was fresh and smelled of herbs. She wondered if he cleaned his teeth with some kind of powdered mixture, as civilized people did.

She waited for a time, but her need was becoming urgent. Gingerly she began to pull the fur away, and then he rolled the other way again, his back to her.

She caught her breath. A long, deep purple scar ran from the nape of his neck down to the small of his back. Perhaps lower. It was thick and ugly, and she wondered how he had been wounded. Who had tended him? She tentatively reached out her fingers.

He rolled back over. There was such a look of joy and wonder on his face that she tingled. He touched his forehead and murmured something in his language. Then he chuckled and exhaled slowly.

He said, "Mahwah, *tahaso*." He made as if to shiver and reached down for the fur.

She cleared her throat. "Ah, sir, I have to . . ." She closed her eyes. Such things were not permitted to be discussed in civilized society.

*Well, this is not civilized society, is it?* she thought in a fit of pique.

In the distance, a whippoorwill sang out its song. Then she felt something tugging on her hair. She opened her mouth to cry out, but remembered just in time that she might lose her tongue. She flipped over on her back, ramming into him, grunting heavily at the pain in her thigh.

Then she would have screamed—no matter the cost—if Wusamequin had not clamped his hand over her mouth.

A tiny creature gazed up at her. It resembled a male human being, except for its size: it stood perhaps six inches tall. It—*he*—was dressed in a skirt of fur, a tiny crown of flowers encircling his brow, and strands of her hair dangled between his hands as if he had been tying up the line of a great brigantine.

As Isabella pushed herself back into Wusamequin's chest, the little man dropped her hair, put his hands on his hips, and laughed at her.

Then another creature popped out of the grass bed. This one was a female, and she wore a leather dress much like Isabella's. Both she and the little man were barefoot, but seemed oblivious to the cold.

"*Makiawisug*," Wusamequin said to her. The two tiny sprites dashed over to him; he put out his hand and they leaped onto it, then cheered in squeaky voices as he raised them to his eye level.

He spoke to them, and each in turn giggled and stared at Isabella. The woman scrambled up Wusamequin's arm, reaching the summit of his shoulder. She reached up to bat both hands against his earbob, making it gently swing. She spoke to the medicine man again, and pointed at Isabella.

Meanwhile, the male sauntered over to her. He folded his arms and inclined his head as he chattered in a high, squeaky voice.

Over her initial shock, she found the pair quite charming. "Little people?" she asked Wusamequin, not taking her eyes off the elfin man. "Leprechauns? Brownies?"

Both of those sorts of Little People were actually quite mischievous, if not malicious. They would curdle milk, rip clothes to tatters. It was even said that they gave human babies to the faery, in return for faery babies, changelings, who were taken in and cared for by their unsuspecting human parents.

Before Wusamequin could answer, a third Makiawisug burst from the grass. Then another one crawled from beneath the tent flap. They both dashed over to Wusamequin, as a child might race to a favorite uncle.

He said something to the quartet; the female slid down his arm to his open palm, jumped off, and landed in the grass. Wusamequin leaned over Isabella and pulled open the entrance to the tent, and the four raced outside.

They quickly returned with a very plain gray bowl, held above their heads as the Indians had carried her father. They set it down in front of her and skittered back, forming a line.

Wusamequin gestured to the bowl. She stared first at it, and then at him. He made as if to lift his breechcloth.

"A chamber pot?" she asked breathlessly. "You want me to . . . to use it? *Here?* In the tent?"

He folded his arms. She scratched her cheek, unsure how to proceed, but knowing that she was running out of time.

After a moment, she extended her hand, pointing to the tent flap. She said, "*Wunneet.*"

His face drew up in an amused smile. He reached for his shirt as he got to his feet. Hunching his shoulders, he chuckled as he left the tent, taking his shirt with him.

The Makiawisug backed away from the bowl, their upturned faces a mixture of curiosity and apprehension. Isabella pointed to the tent flap and said, "Away. I am a lady."

The foursome burst into merry giggles and decamped, dashing off after Wusamequin.

Feeling incredibly awkward, Isabella heeded the call of nature, lifted up the side of the tent, and dumped the bowl out onto the grass.

She reasoned that Wusamequin, too, had morning oblations to fulfill, so she lay back down. She was thirsty and hungry. Her leg was sore, but as she pulled up her dress and examined it, she noted that the proud flesh—the area that swelled around a wound—had become less puffy. She was continuing to heal.

The flap opened and Wusamequin entered with two bowls, one in each hand. The four little people rode on his shoulders, swinging their legs in a carefree, easy manner. The little female smiled at Isabella and got to her feet, standing on tiptoe to grab at Wusamequin's earbob. He tilted his head obligingly, and she whispered in Wusamequin's ear. He blushed. Isabella was stunned. She would never have imagined Wusamequin capable of blushing.

The female noticed it, too. She pointed at the

color in his cheek and laughed, a shimmering sound that sent a ripple through Isabella. She found herself smiling as the three little men joined in, all four of them squeaking like mice.

The medicine man flashed her a crooked smile as he crossed his ankles and lowered himself to the floor. Isabella was fascinated by the ease with which he moved. It was as if natural laws did not apply to him; he was like a spirit of the air.

"*Aquai*," he said to her. She realized it was a greeting.

"*Aquai*," Isabella replied.

Pleased, he nodded. "*Quin'a month'ee?*"

She hesitated. In polite society, he would be asking after her health. She took a breath and answered, "*Wunneet. Wneeweh.*"

His smile brightened up the tent. He handed her one of the bowls and said, "*Kschittau.*"

Now she was at a loss; she had no idea what he had said. She pointed to the bowl and said, "Porridge? *Kschittau?*" for it appeared to be something made out of cornmeal.

The dainty female scurried down his arm and gestured for Isabella to lower her bowl. She did so, and the tiny maid began to vigorously blow on the porridge.

"Hot!" Isabella cried.

"*Kschittau*," the little maid said, clapping her hands. She danced in a circle and blew on the porridge some more.

"*Wneeweh*," Isabella said to her.

"Mahwah," Wusamequin cut in, "learn the

People's language. Makiawisug help Mahwah."

"You are to be my tutors," Isabella said to the little maid. The creature turned to Wusamequin, who spoke to her. She turned back to Isabella and clapped her hands.

"*Nia ktachwahnen,*" the female chirped. The three tiny men fell into laughter. Isabella looked from them to Wusamequin, who was shaking his head. The maid gestured to the medicine man and repeated the phrase. The men were still laughing, and Isabella was abashed.

"I have no idea what you're saying," she told her. "But I know that you're playing a trick on me."

Her voice set the four into gales of laughter, the female enjoying herself so thoroughly that she collapsed on the bed of grass and rolled from side to side.

Wusamequin spoke to her again, a trifle more sharply this time, and the female lay on the grass giggling. Then she galloped over to Isabella and made a show of straightening the hem of Isabella's dress. She called over her companions, and together they retied the lacings of her mocassins. Then the little maid turned to Wusamequin, asking him a question.

He answered her, and she darted out of the tent, calling to one of the three fellows to accompany her. Isabella frowned quizzically; Wusamequin leaned back on one arm and sipped his porridge. He seemed quite content, the lord of the manor, taking his ease.

*Don't forget he is a savage,* she reminded herself. *He has never been inside a real home.*

133

She sipped delicately at her own bowl of porridge, reminding herself that she was a lady and she must continue to behave as one. Perhaps she would be able to set an example for him, show him how to comport himself so that one day, he might be presentable in society. . . .

*And on what occasion would he be presented?* a voice inside her mind asked mockingly. *What possible reason would this primitive have to mingle with his betters?*

Petulantly, she set down her porridge and said, "Please, may I have some water? I'm terribly thirsty."

He cocked an eyebrow at her. *"Menachk?"*

"Oh, I don't remember how you say it. Are you telling me to say 'please'? Is that the word for 'water?'" She ran her fingers through her hair, finding mats and tangles, and no evidence anywhere of a comb—further proof that she was living among savages. "I should like water," she said imperiously. "Wa-ter."

"Wusamequin speaks Yangees, Mahwah," he reminded her. His brows were knit. She could see he was confused by her iciness. *What do you expect?* she wanted to demand of him. *Do you think it pleases me to be your prisoner?*

A silence fell between them. He shrugged and went back to sipping his porridge.

"You are impertinent," she shot at him. "I cannot get my own drink, and yet you deny me a simple drink of water, when at home I should have cream if I wish. I am a lady, sir."

"You are a slave," he replied flatly.

Then he rose and stomped out of the tent, nearly stepping on the four Makiawisug as they carried in a pumpkin-colored gourd sloshing with water. They cried out in one voice as his moccasin nearly crushed them; Wusamequin stepped around them and left the tent.

"Good riddance to bad company," Isabella hissed. She reached for the water gourd and took a good, hefty swallow, allowing it to run down her chin in a way that was not at all proper or civilized. She didn't care. She drank some more, draining the gourd, and then she wiped her mouth with the back of her hand.

The little female climbed up onto her lap. She took both her hands and trailed them down Isabella's hand and began to sing to her. Her strange little voice took on a lilting, soft melody, almost like a lullaby.

"You're very kind," she said. "Not like him at all."

But that wasn't true. He had been kind to her. More than kind. He had saved her life.

"He is a savage," she said aloud.

And she had no idea why that made her feel so miserable.

# ❖ Chapter Eleven ❖

*I* had a clear and detailed spirit dream, Wusamequin thought happily. *As my father did before me. I have begun to grow as a medicine man!*

*Mahwah brought me luck.*

With Great Bear guiding him, as he had guided Wusamequin into the forest, Wusamequin had dreamed of a magical, safe place for the People of the River. It had shimmered with rainbows, and gleamed with purity.

*This is your refuge*, the enormous bear had assured his human nephew.

Perhaps clairvoyance, then, was Wusamequin's special gift. Shamans such as he sought their talents, and it was a fine day when they learned what they were. He could command light and dark, after a fashion. He suspected he had some control of the weather, but he was not yet certain of that. He had already known he was a good healer—look at Mahwah—and the manner in which he healed, by fighting the demons within one's sick spirit, was clairvoyance of a sort.

Whatever the case, he was bursting with pride when he conferred with Oneko and told him of the dream. The sachem was well pleased; and the second day of flight brought the People to the waterfall of his dream. Strong waters roared over a cliff and rushed in a wide, burbling river toward lakes and streams far distant. The water was strikingly blue. It was clean and sweet. Perhaps this water had never tasted the lips of a white skin on its surface.

Fortunate waterfall.

Oneko and Sasious stood with Wusamequin, where they had a good view of the land around the falls. Wusamequin said, "In my dream, there were caves behind the falls. Great Bear said we should live there, concealed from the eyes of the Yangees, until the danger is past. The falling water will eat the smoke of our cooking fires. We will be safe."

Oneko pursed his lips and raised his brows, clearly impressed. "You dreamed this very place?"

Wusamequin nodded. "Great Bear guided me here."

Sasious shifted his weight and gripped his toma-hawk. Wusamequin doubted that the war chief was unaware of the signals he was sending: apprehension, distrust. He liked Wusamequin less than he had the day before, or the day before that. Being set apart by strong feelings was a common situation for a medi-cine man; he walked with spirits and he possessed powers, both of which frightened most people. But his relationship with Sasious was more complex.

One thing Wusamequin could not do was con-trol other people; and so he concentrated on what his sachem had to say, and ignored what Sasious was trying to say.

"Did Great Bear tell you that the People will stay here long?"

Wusamequin shook his head. "He didn't know. That remains for us to decide."

Oneko nodded. The feathers in his hair ruffled in the breeze. He had lived a long time, and he counted coup with pride. Wusamequin revered and honored him.

"How is the wound of the hostage?" Oneko asked. "Is her spirit still troubled?"

"Yes," Wusamequin replied. "I battled in the spirit world on her behalf, but it'll take a while for her to heal."

Oneko and Sasious drew back slightly, a common reaction when Wusamequin discussed invisible matters. "Did you prevail?"

"I prevailed."

"Her presence is upsetting the People," Oneko went, his gaze shifting from Wusamequin's face to Sasious's and back again. "I'm beginning to rethink my decision to keep her with us. Perhaps it would be better to sell her to *les Français*. Then the Yangees may forget about us."

Wusamequin shook his head. "If her father lives and makes it back to the Yangees, he'll tell them that we killed the soldiers. They'll want revenge."

Sasious spit into the water, which deeply

offended Wusamequin. The waters were to be kept clean for the next seven generations. The People had the obligation to conduct themselves as guardians, not despoilers, as the white skins did. He concealed his reaction as the war chief continued, "Let them come. We'll scalp them all, warriors, women, and children."

"Wusamequin shares your hatred," Oneko reminded him. "In this, the sons of our People are brothers. But this girl poses a dilemma that goes beyond satisfying our hatred. If she draws the Yangees to us, that's bad. But if she is our only shield against their wrath . . ."

"She only serves as a shield as long as she remains with us," Sasious contended. "If we hand her over either to les Français or to the Yangees, the Yangees will war on us because they won't fear that harm will come to her."

"If we keep her too long, they'll attempt to rescue her," Oneko countered.

"But only if they find us," Wusamequin reminded them both. "I'll work to create strong medicine to hide the People from the Yangees."

"Do you have such medicine now?" Oneko asked, impressed.

"No," Wusamequin admitted. "But I'll put my entire spirit to work on it."

Oneko smiled grimly. "I have faith in you, my young shaman. See that you do that." He cocked his head. "If protecting the white skin maiden is a burden to you—"

Sasious brightened, and Wusamequin said quickly, "It's not."

"Her presence in his wigwam concerns me," Sasious said, his voice lilting with concern as he frowned anxiously at Wusamequin. His eyes were wide with "worry," and the scar across his mouth angled like a broken arrow as he pursed his lips. "The spirit warrior needs to walk alone; he shouldn't have any distractions. Besides, if she sees him performing his spells, she may steal his medicine and use it against us."

Oneko looked thoughtful. "Those are good points." He put his hand on Sasious's shoulder. "Well said, my war chief." The wind ruffled the feathers in his hair as he looked at Wusamequin. "What do you say, my medicine warrior?"

"I wish her to remain in my wigwam," Wusamequin replied. "I ask this of Oneko." He lowered his head in his leader's direction to indicate that he would accept the sachem's decision, whatever it might be.

The roar of the falls was the only sound for three or four heartbeats. Wusamequin kept his gaze averted; but it was a politeness. His obedience to the ways of his people kept him in check. Sasious was stronger than Oneko, and Wusamequin was magically more powerful. But both of them owed Oneko their respect, and their allegiance. Unless the sachem had the full support of both his lieutenants, he couldn't effectively govern.

*But if Oneko orders her from my protection, what shall I do?* He thought of her bad behavior with a mixture of anger and pity. *Mahwah's foolish to put herself away from me. I am the only friend she has in this place, and many wish her dead.*

*I should wish her dead as well. I have no understanding why my heart is not hard against her. Perhaps she is a witch, and has enchanted me. I should discuss this with Great Bear.*

The waters roared. Above their heads, a scattering of passenger pigeons flapped through the blue. During Mahwah's healing ceremony, Wusamequin had painted his face blue with black dots, to remind Mahwah's spirit of freedom. The demon on her chest had sought to imprison her in sorrow and despair by entrapping her in memories of the past.

He knew that prison well.

Sasious subtly shifted his weight, as if to remind Oneko that the sachem was taking a long time to render his decision. It was rude, but a war chief had more leeway than a spirit warrior to behave aggressively. His heart was about battles and winning. Wusamequin's was also, but against very different enemies.

After a time, Oneko said, "We'll keep things as they are. For now."

Sasious clenched his jaw and wrapped his fingers around his tomahawk, his body poised as if for further argument, but he said nothing in response.

Wusamequin stood down as well. He had gotten what he wanted.

Oneko crossed his arms over his chest to signal that he was moving on. "War chief, ask your braves to find the caves behind the falls. Wusamequin, assist them." He raised a hand as if to answer Wusamequin's next question. "I'll take charge of Mahwah until your return."

"She's not one of us, and that is not her name," Sasious said angrily, releasing some of his frustration at not being awarded custody of her. But at a stern look from Oneko, he added, "But if Oneko wishes her to be called in the manner of Beautiful, then I'll do as he wishes."

"My heart soars at your acquiescence," Oneko said flatly, raising his chin. He stood every inch a leader, and Wusamequin saw how his spirit shone. He knew the People were lucky that he wore the beaded belt of office.

Wusamequin said to Oneko, "I know exactly where the caves are. Great Bear and I walked inside them in my dream. When Sasious gives the word, we can be off to survey them."

Pleased and surprised, Oneko smiled and raised his brows. "Is that so, my son? Then I'll tell the People to begin preparations to descend the cliffs."

"We should check first," Sasious objected. "To make sure his dream was true."

Oneko shook his head. "I have faith in Wusamequin." He put his hand on Wusamequin's shoulder and smiled at him. "Please thank Great Bear for us."

Wusamequin was grateful for the show of support. And thrilled that the nature of his shamanic gift was so clear to him. He inclined his head and said, "I will thank him."

Not able to learn if the four little people had names, Isabella decided to name them after the fairy creatures in *A Midsummer Night's Dream*, a play about magic by Englishman William Shakespeare. The little female Makiawisug was therefore Titania, the Queen of the Fairies. The man who appeared to be her consort was Oberon, the King. The other two were Puck and Cobweb.

After leaving the tent for a short time, Titania and Oberon had returned dragging a human-sized comb made of tortoise shell like a *travois* behind them. After some gesticulation, Isabella had understood that Titania wished her to lie down. Then she and Oberon worked the comb together, rather like two people hoeing fields, and ran it through Isabella's hair. When they hit a mat, they would stop combing and busily set to work untangling it.

*I should be called Cobweb*, Isabella thought. Having her hair combed was sheer heaven, and with a smile upon her face, Isabella began to doze.

The sound of footfalls in the moist earth outside the tent roused her; she startled and sat up. Still working with the comb, Titania and Oberon squeaked in protest as the pair swung in a wide semicircle. She carefully cupped her hand around them, and they dropped into her palm.

She lowered them to her lap and watched the tent flap. Puck and Cobweb ran toward it, hunkering down to see who was coming. She tensed; she had been rude to Wusamequin, and she didn't know what to expect. It had been stupid of her; she had better make amends to him, for she sensed that he stood between her and Sasious.

Oneko, the chief of the savages, lifted up the flap and peered in at her. Isabella gasped and put her hand to her throat. She panicked, and glanced at Titania, who watched her with curious brown eyes.

Oneko ignored the tiny fairy queen as he came into the tent, speaking to Isabella in his native tongue. Isabella tried to stand up, but her thigh pained her and she stayed where she was. Her mind raced; her heart skipped beats.

Finally, she rasped out, "*Aquai.*"

The chief smiled kindly at her. "*Aquai,* Mahwah."

He walked toward her, raising his moccasin and almost planting it directly on Puck. Isabella cried out, "Oh, please, do be careful!"

Oneko froze. He looked down at the ground and then back up at her, a quizzical look on his face. Puck scurried out of his way, burying himself in the grass bed.

Isabella cleared her throat. "Excuse me, sir," she said to Oneko. "I—I feared for the little man." She tried to remember the word. "Makiawisug."

The man's lips parted and his brows shot up. He said something to her that sounded like a question. When she shyly shook her head to indicate that she didn't understand, he said slowly, "Makiawisug?"

Titania threw her hands in the air and trilled her musical laughter. The three little men guffawed, pointing at Oneko and making terrible faces at him.

"Yes," she said in English.

He was shocked. She could find no other word for it. He looked around the tent, his gaze passing right over all four of the little people.

*He cannot see them,* she realized. *And it surprises him that I can. Perhaps that's a bad thing.*

So she laughed and said, "I was only joking!" She knew he couldn't understand her but she hoped he would discern her meaning from her tone of voice.

Smiling uncertainly, he crossed his legs at the ankles and lowered himself to the floor, not quite as agile as Wusamequin, but nimble for a man of years. He put his hands on his knees and stared hard at her. She looked around for something to offer him, and lifted the water gourd, which still had a bit of water in it.

He raised a brow, and she found herself thinking of her father. A lump formed in her throat as she reminded herself that though this man was perhaps her father's age, he was nothing like her father. They said in Albany that Indians stole white babies, ripped open their throats, and drank their blood. They said they . . . they took advantage of Englishwomen, as Sasious had tried to do.

The hand she held out to him began to tremble violently. She wasn't certain what to do; if she withdrew the gourd, she might offend him. But she had begun to shake so badly that she was afraid all the water would slosh out, or that she would drop the gourd.

Slowly he reached out and took the gourd. His fingertips brushed hers, and she jerked. His mouth drooped as if in displeasure. She tried to swallow, but she couldn't. Her mouth felt as if she had drunk deeply of dust, not water.

He silently drank, watching her. The four little people piled onto her lap, Titania stroking her fingers as if for comfort. Then Titania curled up like a cat, singing to herself.

Oneko saw none of that.

"Mahwah," he said. He began speaking to her in a low, steady voice. She didn't understand a word, but she listened hard. It was no good. Tears welled; she was tired and frightened and she wished Wusamequin would come back. Had she been placed in Oneko's care? What was happening?

He stopped speaking. She didn't know what to do. She had already been criticized for staring at him. She didn't know if he wanted her to answer him, or perform some task, or simply sit there.

Titania sat up and looked at Isabella. "Mahwah," she said, and pointed to her wounded thigh. Then she gestured to her own dress of leather and fringes and rolled up the hem, exposing her upper leg.

"Oh." Isabella flushed crimson. Surely he did not wish her to show him her wound! It would be so unseemly.

Titania repeated the motion and jumped out of Isabella's palm. Isabella took a breath and reached for the hem of her dress. Titania gestured eagerly for her to continue.

Dutifully, she rolled up the hem and pushed down her legging, so embarrassed she could barely breathe.

He leaned forward, studying it. She saw that he was examining the packing and the stitches. He looked most intrigued. Then he sat back, and spoke to her again.

Titania stretched her arms toward the tent flap. Footfalls thudded outside, and there was talking. Isabella inhaled sharply, and the man spoke to her again.

"Wusamequin?" she asked hopefully. Had he told Oneko he no longer wished to endure her company? Was someone coming for her? Someone . . . else?

The tent flap opened and a brave she didn't know poked his head in and spoke to Oneko. Before Isabella had a chance to react, Oneko came forward and scooped her up in his arms. As he did so, Titania screeched, clinging to Isabella's palm as she was jostled to and fro. The little men also scrambled for purchase, rolling in the valley of her dress as Oneko carried her out of the tent.

Outside, four braves in leather jerkins and leggings waited with a litter, which had been constructed of a rectangle of leather bound around two long, straight tree branches. Oneko deposited her on it. She tried to tuck her legs beneath herself but her thigh hurt too much, so she kept that leg extended while she bent her knee and slipped her ankle under the other knee. Then she leaned back on her hands.

One of the braves glared at her, showing his teeth like an angry dog. She looked questioningly back at Oneko, who had not seen. He waved his hand and the four braves moved off, walking toward the fire rings she had seen the night before. There were only embers now, and many of the tents had been taken down. Women and men were in the process of dismantling the ones that still stood.

Her small procession caused a stir as Oneko led the way past the busy villagers. She wondered why he hadn't ordered her put back in her *travois*.

Birds sang; the tall pines trembled with movement as squirrels capered along the branches. Clouds hung in an azure sky.

After a few minutes, a mighty rush of water soon overpowered all other sounds; to her right, a waterfall far more massive than the one she had seen on the forest path cascaded in a horseshoe, rushing and tumbling into whitewater that shot past boulders and overhanging trees. She had never seen such a sight, and despite her situation, she leaned over the side of the litter, caught up in the display of nature's might. Surely the Creator of such thunderous wonder could look after one as small and defenseless as she.

The braves continued to the right. There was a series of rocks that jutted out like the steps of a stairway, and they carefully bore her down them. She saw that the steps descended halfway down the side of the cliff . . . and that approximately fifty feet below them, someone was emerging from behind the falls.

It was Wusamequin, and as he appeared, he looked straight up at her. Her heart leapt; and before she could stop herself, she lifted her hand in a gesture of greeting.

He did not respond. He continued to gaze in her direction, almost as if he didn't see her. Afraid-of-Everything trotted up behind him, stationing himself against his master's leg as the medicine man folded his arms, watching as the braves brought her toward him. The force of the air tossed his long hair as the falls tumbled to the depths below. His features were shadowed, but she could easily make them out. She had learned his face by heart.

Once at his level, he gestured for them to follow. From her new vantage point, she saw that a ledge extended from behind the falls; and the water arched in such a way as to make walking on the ledge possible. The stones were wet, and sheened with moss and slime; and Isabella looked with apprehension at the brave who had glared at her. He was grinning at her as if to say, *I wonder what would happen if I slipped. It seems to me that you would be catapulted into the falls.*

She sincerely doubted that anyone would survive such an ordeal.

Her fingers grew numb as she worked her hands into the leather upon which she sat. The four Makiawisug chattered among each other, quite animated. Then Oberon jumped to his feet, cupped his hands around his mouth, and bellowed at Wusamequin.

Immediately, Wusamequin turned around. Isabella raised her brows. It should have been impossible for Wusamequin to hear the little man's voice, and yet obviously he had. As Wusamequin cocked his head, Oberon pointed at Isabella and nattered on. Wusamequin walked toward the litter, and Isabella licked her lips, at once both anxious and eager for him to draw near.

He spoke to the brave who had glared at her. The man flashed the shaman a guilty look, then moved aside. Wusamequin took his place at the litter, wrapping his hand around the tree branch, and spoke sternly to the others.

The litter moved forward. The displaced brave stomped back toward the rock stairway. Titania darted to Wusamequin's hand and happily petted the back of it with both her tiny hands. Oberon grinned up at Isabella, nodding his head. No one else took the slightest notion of them. They were invisible to everyone except her and Wusamequin.

*They warned him that I was in danger from that brave,* she realized. *They are his friends.*

*They are my friends. I wonder if they would help me escape.*

The thought made her dizzy. She had no idea how she would manage to ask them, or if they would tell Wusamequin, or what he would do if he found out. But she said in a heartfelt voice, "*Wneeweh.*"

Perhaps it was her accent, but they fell to giggling, and would not stop until Wusamequin spoke sharply to them. Then the quartet sat straight up, legs criss-crossed and arms folded across their chests. They were like naughty schoolchildren who had been called to order by their master. Or so Isabella assumed; she had never gone to a school. She had been tutored at home.

Wusamequin spoke to the three other bearers, and the litter turned to the left. There was an opening in the rock face behind the falls broad enough for perhaps six men to enter if they walked shoulder to shoulder.

They carried her through the opening and into a tunnel that extended for perhaps twenty feet. Then it opened up into a vast cavern that had been illuminated with two or three dozen torches. Rock formations hung from the cavernous ceiling like chandeliers; others fanned across the room like the pipes of an organ. Sections of the walls shimmered in the firelight as if they had been created from crystal. They were multicolored—pink and jade and a bluish gray. In the ground, mud of rainbow hues bubbled in small pools—purple and crimson and midnight blue.

The place was of such exquisite beauty that Isabella cried out aloud. She startled the men; one of them chuckled, but was silenced by a look from Wusamequin.

Then he directed the others to move to the right, and they carried her across the vast floor to another small cavelike entrance. They stopped before it; Wusamequin let go of the litter, lifted her against his chest, and carried her into the cave. Afraid-of-Everything chuffed softly behind them, his paws padding on the hard packed ground. Her four tiny friends scrambled off her and climbed onto Wusamequin's shoulders. He ignored them.

The cavelike entrance opened into another tunnel; also illuminated. As he cornered her, Isabella breathed in his familiar smell. She was slightly more at ease in his arms than she had been in Oneko's, but it didn't matter how she felt. She had no say.

# ❖Chapter Twelve❖

The tunnel opened up into a naturally formed chamber. Wusamequin carried her inside.

She caught her breath. Crimson and indigo flowers hung from the ceiling, and brilliant yellow and purple ones kissed with white. They dangled from vines, as if they were growing down from the earth above them. The walls were gray rock; on them, symbols had been painted in red, white, brown, and black: birds, snakes, and stick figures surrounded by small dots, as if they were glowing. Blankets covered the ground, and there was an array of dishes steaming with delicious-smelling food positioned in a semicircle. In the center of the room, a fire burned brightly as it devoured small chunks of wood. Isabella looked up, and saw no hole for the smoke to escape. And yet, the room was not smoky at all.

She saw that the perimeter of the chamber was lined with flowers; she didn't know if they had been placed there deliberately or if they were growing there. The effect was enchanting, and very much as she had pictured Titania's fairy bower in William Shakespeare's play.

*"Komeekha,"* he said, his voice strained and polite,

as he set her down on a colorful blanket beside the fire. The four fairy people scampered out of her lap and ran to explore, sniffing at the food and looking expectantly up at Wusamequin. He spoke to them, and they shifted their gaze to Isabella.

"Wusamequin," she began, playing with the hem of her dress as she looked up at him. "I'm sorry I was rude. Please accept my apology."

He folded his arms across his chest. He glanced toward the tunnel, and then he tapped his fingers together.

A thick shadow played over the entrance to the chamber, obscuring it from the view of anyone who should come down the tunnel.

Startled, she glanced from it to him. His face remained impassive.

Then he settled down beside her, and took her left hand in his left hand. His cleared his throat.

"Listen to my words," he said; and as always, it startled her when he spoke in her tongue. "The Makiawisug are the slaves of Mahwah now."

"We don't keep slaves," she replied, but her face tingled. That was untrue. The English imported slaves from Africa; however, the Colonists had begun to make slavery illegal within some of their borders. She wondered if that had anything to do with the fact that the savages were beginning to do the work for the Colonials that the slaves had once performed, in return for provisions and clothing.

She lowered her head and said, "*Wneeweh.*" She

looked at the little people, who were still hovering around the dishes, and said, "*Gemeze.*" They tucked into the dishes, scooping up stew with their tiny hands.

A ghost of a smile flashed over Wusamequin's features as he watched them, and she relaxed a trifle. Then he said, "I will fight the evil spirit again."

He spread the forefinger and middle finger of his right hand wide, then drew them down over her eyebrows, urging her to close her eyes. Reluctantly she complied, then opened them again, to find him staring at her. She grimaced; he smiled, and closed his eyes while she watched.

So she closed them again.

"Listen to your heart," he told her.

He began to chant very softly. She could barely hear the words, but they seemed to summon a new rhythm into her pulse. She grew alarmed; she was the daughter of a physician, and she knew that an irregular heartbeat was rarely a good thing. Yet she kept her eyes closed and listened.

Warmth diffused throughout her body, and she found herself smiling. Wusamequin's voice rose and fell, so quietly that at times she thought he had stopped singing. Then her ear would catch his voice again, and after a few minutes she felt lighter, as if she were beginning to float off the ground. His hand around hers ceased to feel like a separate thing; she lost track of where she began and he left off.

Her mind wandered as she wondered what her little band of four were doing; as if he knew she had stopped concentrating, Wusamequin gave her hand a squeeze.

His voice rose and fell, rose and fell; the fire crackled. She smelled first the succulent food, and then the sweetness of the flower blossoms, which reminded her of her mother's perfume.

Her throat tightened as the image of her mother filled her mind. The warmth seeped away, and she began to flood with grief.

As if in response, Wusamequin gripped her hand harder and raised his voice. Isabella's viewpoint shifted; she saw her own self, nigh these ten months, racing into her mother's bedroom.

There was her mother dead in her bed, and everything in her cried out, "No! No, Mama! Oh, please, no!"

Wusamequin inhaled sharply, held his breath, and exhaled. His chant rose in pitch and shifted in rhythm. He clamped his hand around hers, and the grief poured out of her as she wept, so hard she made no sound.

He held her hand, then pulled her into his arms and cradled her against his chest.

*Mama, Mama, Mama . . .*

His heart spoke the word against her ear, and as she listened it became, *My son, my son, my son . . .*

She whispered, "You have lost someone, too. Your child."

And she saw in her mind a tiny copper-hued baby, fists clenched, arms flailing. A hand wrapped around the baby's right fist; it was small and feminine. Another hand wrapped around his left. It was larger and heavily veined, and Isabella knew it for Wusamequin's.

"You have a wife," she murmured, feeling dashed. "Where is she?"

And then she knew. She knew that they were dead. She was afraid to know more.

So she closed her mind against the images, even those of her mother.

He chanted on; she wondered if the others would come looking for him. That thought faded, replaced by an anxious thought of Sasious.

He sang on.

The warmth returned, and the sensation of floating; her errant thoughts vanished.

Her wounded thigh grew very warm, then tingled; then was overlaid with a refreshing coolness, as if she had just stepped from a bath. It was quite pleasant; she began to open her eyes and he squeezed her hand tightly, as if to remind her not to. She obeyed, though she was horribly tempted.

The chant rose, fell. Her mind drifted to her father; she wondered where he was, if he was alive. If he would come for her.

*Not if. When.*

*What if he never does? What if I am trapped with these primitives forever?*

She reeled, as if she were jumping off the cliff outside.

Wusamequin's voice rose, and he squeezed her hand, but it did no good. She had lost the thread of his song, and her heart rattled with fear.

She began to open her eyes; then she felt his other hand pressed against them, forcing them closed. He kept singing.

And she saw him in her mind's eye as she had seen him before, half-naked but for a loincloth. This time he held a scalping knife, and he was circling the fire at the center of the chamber they sat in, only she was not there.

A tall misshapen creature with a topknot joined the circle around the fire, sitting back on muscular haunches, extending long arms that looked like claws. Its fanged mouth dripped with saliva; its red eyes gleamed and it spread wide its clawed hands, swiping the air between them.

She moaned, frightened. Wusamequin kept his hand over her eyes, holding her other one. He chanted.

In her mind, he flung himself through the fire and at the monster. It was unprepared and staggered backward. Flailing at the spirit warrior, it growled with fury as Wusamequin grabbed its topknot and hacked it off. He threw it in the fire, and the demon howled in protest, lunging to grab it out of the flames.

Wusamequin took advantage of its distraction to leap onto its back. He grabbed one ear and sliced it off, tossing it into the fire. He hacked off the other one. He wrapped both his hands around the knife, raising it over his head, preparing to plunge it into the neck of the fearsome creature. But the monster whirled around expectantly, trying to grab him; Wusamequin hung onto his back and rode him like a wild horse he was attempting to tame.

And suddenly Isabella's mind filled with memories of Albany, and of the sunny day her father and mother had taken her to the commons, to view a dozen horses being trained for regimental service. On the sweet green grass, several young soldiers had erected a practice ring of white-painted wood. They'd run the horses inside the ring and, dressed in their white breeches and red coats, they were attempting to convince them that they should allow double bridles and cavalry saddles. Older, perhaps wiser soldiers perched on the railings, watching and laughing.

Civilians approached to enjoy the spectacle, and spectacle it was. The feisty steeds bucked and stamped their hooves, tossing their manes as the young men chased after them. Their white breeches soon became brown with dirt and streaked with grass stains.

James Stout, an enterprising innkeeper, had his barmaids bring out tankards of ale to sell. Soon, meat pies were offered as well; it became quite a festival. Isabella nearly swooned with the happy memory. Her mother, dressed exquisitely in China blue, twirled her parasol as her father doffed his tricorne and bade Mrs. DeWitt a lovely day.

Her happiness transformed into longing, and then into fear. What if she never saw that world again?

*Papa, Papa, come for me. Save me. Bring me back. Find me!*

Then the memory vanished as if someone had snatched it away from her. In its place, the battle between the demon and Wusamequin took a sudden turn as the monster reached around and grabbed Wusamequin's leg. As Isabella watched in horror, it tore the medicine man off its back and held him out over the fire. One of his moccasins began to smoke.

Wusamequin shouted in pain, and Isabella screamed.

Then she darted forward, grabbed Wusamequin's knife from his hand, and stabbed the monster in the arm. It threw back its head and bellowed in agony. Its grip on Wusamequin slackened, and Isabella grabbed his arm and tried to push him out of the fire as he fell.

She was partially successful; his foot came down hard on the end of a piece of wood that had not begun to burn. It flipped up into the air, then fell into the fire, sending up flames and sparks.

As he struggled to find his balance, the demon batted a claw across his chest, sending him flying across the room. He slammed into the gray stone wall and slid to the ground, bringing a vine of flowers with him.

With the shaman out of the fray, the monster whirled on Isabella, who screamed again, backing away. It came for her, wildly waving its arms. Its mouth opened and its fangs gleamed in the firelight. Its crimson eyes glowed.

She backed away, horrified, unable to tear her gaze away from the hideous thing.

As if from far away she heard Wusamequin chanting, and felt his work-roughened hand across her eyes.

Then in the next breath, both the chanting and his hand were gone.

She looked over at him, to see that he had gotten to his feet again. He held out his hands and shouted, "Knife, Mahwah!"

The monster's fetid breath wafted over her like steam from a kettle; overwhelmed, she staggered backward, clutching the knife in both her hands.

"Knife!" Wusamequin bellowed as he approached the creature on its left flank.

"No, no," she pleaded, unable to give it up. The demon spread wide its arms, the injured one dripping blood, and rushed at her.

With a shriek, she threw the knife under its arm to the shaman, who grabbed it. With a fierce war cry, he stabbed the demon under its arm, ducking as it whirled in his direction. The force of his movement extracted the knife; he landed on the balls of his feet and propelled himself back toward the demon. This time the knife sank into its chest.

Isabella cried out and ran forward, pounding at the bleeding monster with her fists. Her hands sank into bloody fur reeking of the grave. She was revolted, but she continued to hit it, as Wusamequin stabbed it over and over again. Blood sprayed everywhere.

Then the creature threw back its head, screaming in agony, and toppled backward, into the fire.

Isabella fell to her knees, sobbing and retching, her hands coated with its blood. Wusamequin hurried to her, bending over her, gathering her up in his arms. He held her as he had held her before, and she buried her face against his chest, coughing and weeping.

"Mahwah," came the voice.

It was darker in the chamber now, but she could still make out Wusamequin's features as he leaned over her. He smelled of steamy warmth, and his hair had been pulled away from his face. It was wet, strands of it breaking loose from its restraint to curl around his temples.

He touched her face, pressing his fingertips against each of her temples, and the hollows of her cheeks. Tension sank away, and she felt herself come back to herself.

He gazed into her eyes, then moved back. He took her arm and helped her sit up. Then he deliberately laid his palm over her thigh. She began to stiffen, expecting it to hurt.

But it didn't.

Amazed, she lifted her dress. The legging had already been moved down her thigh, exposing the wound.

The swelling was completely gone, and a scab had formed over the entire area, about the size of her fist.

"Oh, my," she murmured. Carefully, she touched it with her fingertips. There was only the slight pressure of her fingers.

She blinked at him. "You healed me."

"Mahwah," he said again. His eyes focused on her, he gracefully rose and took off his shirt. Then he turned his back to her.

She caught her breath. The dark, ugly scar on his back had been transformed. It was thinner, much lighter.

"How . . . ?" she began.

He replied, "You healed me."

They stared at each other in wonder.

"How is that possible?" she asked. "How could I?"

He lowered his shirt and turned back to face her. "The evil spirit. You fought with me."

"But . . . but that was a lot of nonsense," she blurted, "brought on by a fever, I suppose. I did . . . I did nothing with you." Her heart thudded in her ears; she was frightened by the proof before her that he was right.

He gestured as if to raise his shirt again, and she stayed his hand. He said, "*Wneeweh*. You are a spirit warrior, Mahwah. You have medicine."

"No," she said quickly. Then she laughed uneasily and said, "But I do hope my father was able to get the medicine to the fort."

His face became stony. It had been the wrong thing to say.

The fairy queen, Titania, tapped his fingers, and

the three little men encircled a clay bowl and made an attempt to lift it from the ground.

With a heavy sigh, Wusamequin took it and drank deeply. Then he offered the gourd to Isabella.

"Water," he said in English. "Drink."

"Back home I never drank water," she murmured, as she accepted it from him and took a long, grateful sip.

He replied quietly, "This is home."

# ✤ Chapter Thirteen ✤

After three more occasions of performing the strange ritual together, Isabella's thigh was thoroughly healed, save for a pink scar. Wusamequin's scar was still visible, but it was very faint.

Other bits of magic invaded their lives: fresh shoots of flowering vines grew from the ceiling until a thick curtain of colorful, fragrant blossoms separated the chamber into two smaller rooms, one for Isabella and one for Wusamequin. There was always food and drink.

At night, he conjured shadows and threw them against the wall, using the images to teach her more of his language. She learned that *stau* meant "fire," and *siipo* was "river."

They would sit side by side on his side of the flower curtain, both cross-legged, as he conjured up a sweet berry drink and small chunks of smoked fish or berries. Together they would sip the juice and nibble the delicacies, as he fanned open his hands and cast sparkling dots on the crystalline walls, which darkened and formed the images to accompany her language lessons. Her four little friends would sit on her knees or her shoulders, playing with her hair or taking bits of food. One night Titania dragged over a gourd filled with what looked like the juice of raspberries, and set to work dipping a piece of leather in it and rubbing it along Isabella's toes. When she was finished, Isabella's toenails gleamed a soft pink, and she giggled at the sight of them.

Wusamequin smiled, too, and said something to Titania. The fairy queen immediately set to painting Isabella's fingernails as well. As she did so, he flung another image on the wall. This one was of a rose, such as Mrs. DeWitt had cultivated back in Albany.

He said, "Mahwah."

*So it means Rose*, she thought. She touched her ears, which had also healed, and thought of Odina, and she was grateful that Wusamequin had sequestered her in this hidden chamber. On the other hand, this hiding place would make it nearly impossible for her father to find her. She suspected that was the primary reason he had brought her here.

She didn't know if the Indians had spotted any British hunting parties looking for her. She also didn't know if Oneko was still thinking of selling her to the French. She lost track of time, and she began to feel panicky inside the small chamber, imagining herself like a firefly trapped inside a bottle for some young child's amusement. She had not seen the sun in days. Had not seen another living person since they had come here. Was this to be her total existence? She could not imagine it.

She began to feel weary most of the time. She

was languishing; to pass the hours, she began to sleep more. Wusamequin watched her but said nothing. He often disappeared, and began to leave for longer and longer periods of time. She would have been lonely, had it not been for her four little friends.

Each time he left, he would point to the shadow at the threshold of the cave, and say to her in English, "Mahwah stay."

He brought her hides to tan, showing her how; he gave her a beautifully beaded leather jerkin to mend with an English needle and thick, dark thread such as she had never seen before. Then he taught her to do beadwork. She beaded a red rose onto her skirt, and he admired it, smiling at her encouragingly.

"Mahwah," she told him.

His answer was to cup her under the chin and echo, "Mahwah."

Then came a time when he left, and did not come back before the fire had died out. The room stayed illuminated—through magic, she supposed—but soon even those lights began to dim. Then all at once, the chamber fell into darkness.

She was alarmed. She sat with her knees drawn beneath her chin, waiting for him to return. When he did not, she started glancing in the direction of the entrance to the chamber—or where she remembered that it stood, as she could no longer see it. She called out his name, but her own voice echoed softly, as if to mock her.

He had told her to stay. But what if something had happened to him?

Her stomach began to growl. Afraid-of-Everything, who had remained with her, as he often did, whimpered and paced in the dark.

*He told you to stay*, she reminded herself. But next, one of the little people crept into her lap and made a sad, low moan.

*Maybe they're hungry.* She said, "*Gemeze?*" Whichever sprite it was tapped eagerly on her palm.

She hesitated. Then she searched in the dark for her tiny friends; accounting for all four of them, she scooped them up and carried them in her left hand, cradled against her chest. Then she said to the wolf, "Let's go," and he brushed up beside her.

She reached out her right hand, feeling for the entrance. The wolf moved its head; she felt a tug on her dress; and realized that he taken part of it into his mouth. He was going to lead her through the tunnel.

*Then it must be all right*, she told herself.

Afraid-of-Everything padded forward. With her arm extended, Isabella moved with him, awkwardly at first, then finding a gait that matched the wolf's. She couldn't see a thing; she had to trust his instincts.

He led her for what seemed like a longer time that it had taken to first enter the chamber. Then a cold wind washed across her face. Gooseflesh prickled her face and arms. The wolf chuffed and moved forward.

A small circle of dark sky was lit up with stars; it

grew as they neared it. Afraid-of-Everything trotted boldly toward it, pulling her along.

He picked up speed and loped outside, into a vast field of snow.

*Snow? Already? Has so much time passed, then?*

The stars above were blazing like comets, flying across the black heavens, then falling and winking out. There must have been fifty of them or more, bursting into brilliance, and then dying.

A silver moon hung low in the sky, not quite yet full; silhouetted against it, Wusamequin glided gracefully, his arms raised over his head, as if he were guiding the stars to earth. As she walked toward him, her moccasins sank into the deep, powdery snow. She saw that they were standing on a hill; a distance below, bright lights flared in the moonlight whiteness, and then went dark. His silhouette was thrown against the sparkling vastness; it was like his shadow plays against the crystalline wall in their chamber, on a grander canvas.

Without turning, he lowered his arms and said, "Mahwah stay."

"I'm sorry," she said. "But I was afraid. And your wolf was unhappy. And the Makiawisug were hungry."

He turned to face her. She expected to see anger there, but instead, his expression was gentle. He bent down and scratched Afraid-of-Everything behind the ears. The wolf wagged his tail and then trotted off.

The four Makiawisug chattered at Wusamequin. He answered, sounding amused, and took them from

Isabella. He placed them on the ground, and they scampered away, dancing away on top of the snow.

He took her left hand and said, "Mahwah, medicine."

She breathed in the cold night and held it. Then she exhaled, and her breath made vapors in the air. She closed her eyes, and he began to chant.

Swaying with his voice, she felt warmth build inside her, then move from her into the world. Something that was not part of her permeated her being, like light. She sensed that it came from him, and felt shy. He squeezed her hand as if he sensed it, and continued to chant.

After a time, he stopped. She opened her eyes.

They stood together in moonlight. The stars hung fixed in the sky; there were no flares of light at the bottom of the hill.

She expected to be cold, but she was not.

Wusamequin closed his eyes. She did the same. They stood in just that way, unmoving, for what seemed like hours.

The dawn broke, the rays of the sun washing the sky with pinks and purples, and then with a gentle yellow glow. The world was hushed, and beautiful.

"Mahwah," Wusamequin said.

"Rose?" she queried.

"Mahwah," he said again, and extending his arm toward the rosy heavens.

"It means 'Pleasing,' then." She flushed, knowing

that it was his name for her.

"Your heart knows," he chided her.

"Beautiful. You have named me Beautiful," she whispered.

"Mahwah," he affirmed.

"*Wneeweh*," she said feelingly.

He turned around, indicating that she should step in the holes he made as he walked. He began to walk back toward the cave entrance Afraid-of-Everything had guided her to, passing by a stand of spruce trees.

Then Odina, Keshkecho, and Wabun-Anung—Wusamequin had taught her their names—stepped from the stand of trees. Odina was carrying a basket of fish. Keshkecho had a tool that resembled a spade, and Wabun-Anung's face was painted with white and black.

All three of them were staring in shock at her. Wabun-Anung spoke to Wusamequin quite angrily, gesturing at Isabella's leg. His reply was measured and calm.

As he spoke, Isabella ticked her glance toward Odina, whose brows were narrowed in suspicious anger. Her jaw was clenched. She was seething.

Wabun-Anung swept past him, maintaining her dignity despite the fact that with each step, she sank knee-deep into the snow. Wusamequin moved up beside her; when Isabella scrambled to keep up with him, he shook his head at her. She was not to walk with him. She was to walk behind him.

She obeyed, flustered and uneasy. Odina and her sister moved on either side of her, crowding her. She kept her gaze on Wusamequin's back, assuring herself that they certainly would not harm her while he was with them.

They walked seemingly forever. She grew tired but did her best to keep up. Odina pointed at her leg as she spoke to Wabun-Anung, who nodded and frowned at Wusamequin.

They did not enter the cave where Afraid-of-Everything had led her out. Instead, they veered off to the right. Soon the tumultuous thunder of the falls blotted out all conversation.

Steam rose off the running water, which glittered like strands of silver chains as it shot down the cliffs. Isabella marveled once more at the beauty of nature in this wild, untamed place.

She was huffing by the time they ascended the stair-like projections of rock that lined the falls. After a time, Odina shoved the basket of fish in her arms. Keshkecho handed her the spade-like implement as well. Free of their burdens, the women moved more quickly, tripping up the stairs behind Wusamequin and Wabun-Anung.

Seeing them, he looked over his shoulder at Isabella, who was struggling with her burdens. She was unaccustomed to physical labor, and she had been cooped up so long in the chamber that she was a little shaky on her feet.

She expected him to take the fish and the spade from

Spirited

her, but he did not. He didn't even look at her again.

*Boor. Uncouth peasant*, she flung at him in her mind. She railed at him, calling him all kinds of names . . . but it wasn't until the five of them had reached the main entrance of the cave that she realized she had yet to call him a savage. The word somehow no longer applied to him.

Once inside the cave, Wabun-Anung pinched Isabella's arm and dragged her toward a semicircle of three tents erected against the back wall. Other Indians looked up from various chores—cooking, mending things—and Isabella had to skip to keep up with the older woman. She glanced anxiously back at Wusamequin, but his face was unreadable.

Wabun-Anung jerked Isabella to a stop. Isabella stood stock still as the woman swept inside the grandest of the tents. She tried to catch Wusamequin's eye, but he still would not look at her.

The woman reemerged with Oneko at her side. The chief stood with his arms folded as his wife spoke to Odina, who marched up to Isabella, yanked up her dress, and pulled down her legging.

Her healed thigh was revealed for all to see.

Questioning faces turned toward Wusamequin.

He spoke calmly. Then Oneko talked to him, gesturing at Isabella. Wusamequin lowered his head.

Then he walked over to Isabella. As she tilted her head back to look up at him, he said, "Wabun-Anung says you are strong enough to work now. No one eats without working. Oneko agrees to this."

Odina flashed her a cruel smile. Isabella said anxiously, "But there are many here who wish me harm."

His expression remained stolid. She couldn't believe he was the same man who had flung starry shadows on the wall; the same man who fought supernatural creatures to keep her from harm, and who had shared his power with her. The man who had named her beautiful.

"Oneko has said that you are well now. If you are harmed, the one who harms you will pay. He says that his truth will be honored."

Then his veneer cracked, and she saw real concern on his face. His forehead was creased; beneath his long nose, he had sucked in his cheeks and clamped his mouth shut. She wouldn't be surprised if he was drawing blood from biting his cheek.

She said to him, "There's something you aren't telling me."

"Oneko has said that our scouts still seek *les Français*. If he can sell you, he may do it after all. He does not want bad blood in the village."

"I am bad blood?" she blurted, but he didn't have to answer. "But . . ."

He held up a hand. "I am the shaman here. Oneko is the sachem."

"Wabun-Anung," she said bitterly.

"The hearts of the women are hard against you," he conceded. "Now, come. You will be safe tonight." He turned to go, indicating that she should follow after him.

*Like a dog,* she thought angrily, as Afraid-of-Everything trotted beside her. *I'll bet he didn't tell them about the scar on his back. That I helped him.*

As they walked through the vast, colorful cavern, a buzz rose up. People gestured toward her. A puffy-eyed woman holding a baby wrapped in a fur gingerly approached, holding the infant out to Wusamequin. Mucus ran from its tiny nose and its breathing was troubled.

Wusamequin halted, took the baby from its mother, and held it in his arms. Isabella could tell that he was asking the mother questions, and that the woman was frantic. Yet his voice remained calm, and the mother began to grow calmer as well. Isabella saw the effect and thought back to the preceding few minutes, when everyone else had been so furious, and he had seemed passive in comparison. She had translated his lack of emotion to mean that he didn't care about her fate. But it was possible that that was his way—to avoid adding fuel to the fire.

He turned to her and said, "Mahwah, go home. Baby has bad spirits. I must stay." He began to say something else, but sighed instead. He said, "Mahwah, go."

She hesitated, afraid to go without him. He spoke to the wolf, whose ears pricked up. Afraid-of-Everything leaned up against Isabella's leg and looked up at her.

"Afraid-of-Everything walks with you."

"I may be of help. My father treated many children

in Albany, and before that, in London, and I . . ."

He gazed hard at her, his dark brown eyes hooded by his eyebrows.

"Very well." She said to the woman, "I hope your baby feels better."

The woman's response was to narrow her eyes and place her hands protectively on the baby's head.

"Silence, Mahwah," he said. "Go."

She understood; the mother was either afraid she would hurt the baby or else simply despised her. The realization stung, but there was nothing to be done about it. The best thing she could do was obey.

Afraid-of-Everything seemed to sense her mood; he moved slightly ahead of her, leading her toward the tunnel. She looked over her shoulder at Wusamequin, but his attention was on the baby. It was as if he had forgotten about her entirely.

*Papa is the same, when he's about his business.*

The wolf escorted her into the tunnel, which was as dark as a tomb. She had a momentary sense of panic, in which she imagined that practically every person in the tribe was lurking in the dark, waiting to strike her down. Afraid-of-Everything nuzzled her hand as if to reassure her that all was well.

They had walked perhaps a dozen paces when suddenly, lit torches appeared on both sides of the tunnel walls. Each was spaced approximately two feet apart, and they brightly lit her way.

The wolf looked up at her as if to say, *You see? He is still looking out for you.*

They hurried down the tunnel and went into the chamber, which burst into glowing light as she crossed the threshold. The hanging vines of flowers had been pulled back from the center and fastened to the walls, so that they resembled curtains. A warm fire danced in the fire ring; surrounding it were gaily colored pieces of leather, upon which over a dozen gourds and bowls brimming with food were arranged.

The four Makiawisug had changed their furs and hides for brilliant flower petals of midnight blue and white; they were dancing around a circlet of exquisite red flowers, the like of which Isabella had never seen before.

When they saw her, they raced toward her, chattering and laughing. Titania said, "*Komeekha!*"

"*Wneeweh,*" Isabella replied. She spread her arms wide to take in the feast. "*Wunneet!*"

"*Gemeze! Menackh!*" Oberon urged her. "*Mattape!*"

"*Qu'in a month'ee?*" Puck queried.

"Are you asking me about Wusamequin?" she asked the little man.

"'*Nia ktachwahnen,*'" Cobweb said in a singsong voice, and the four set to laughing.

Her cheeks warmed; she knew they were teasing her but she had no idea what they were saying.

She crossed her ankles and slowly sank to the earth. She peered at the many dishes of food, her mouth watering. Then her lips parted in astonishment as her gaze dropped upon what could only be a dish of trifle—berries and sponge cake and a froth of cream. She smelled the sherry in the blend.

*Where did he find this?* she thought wonderingly. Her mind raced. *Is my father here? Did he prepare it?*

But she knew the answer: Wusamequin had created it for her, by magic.

Tears of gratitude welled in her eyes. She picked up the heavenly confection and held it against her chest.

"*Wneeweh*, Wusamequin," she said.

She tucked into the food with gusto. Now and then she glanced into the tunnel, hoping that he would come. But he did not.

The four fairy people danced and sang to her, and she felt her eyes growing heavy. After a time she gave in to her desire to sleep, and crawled into her soft bed. Afraid-of-Everything curled up beside her. That was not his custom; he usually slept on the other side of the vine partition with his master.

Isabella soon sank into a deep slumber. As she slept, the fire crackled and the four Makiawisug curled in her hair and at her elbow. Titania's lips brushed her cheek. The chamber grew hushed with the sibilant breathing of the sleepers.

# ❖ Chapter Fourteen ❖

Isabella slept she knew not for how long. Then suddenly she shot into awareness. On the wall, Wusamequin's form hovered before her. His face was pinched with misery; he was holding the baby in his arms, and it was limp and gray.

Behind him, two wolves threw back their heads and howled like the dread Banshee of Ireland, said to herald untimely death.

"Oh, no!" Isabella cried as she ran to the image. Without thinking, she reached out a hand and touched Wusamequin's face. "It cannot be!"

His face was as solid as if he stood before her. She jerked her hand away, then touched his cheek, tears welling in her eyes.

He did not seem as shocked as she did; then he held the baby out to her. She took it, cradling it in her arms. The little thing was not dead, but breathing very faintly. Its mouth was slack.

"Mahwah," Wusamequin said. He held out his left hand.

She took it.

And at once, she and he were charging through a forest, he with a bow and arrow, she carrying a spear.

179

Their feet flew over brush and brambles. Ahead of them raced a demon much like the one they had routed; it was flying over the ground, shrieking and cackling like a mad thing.

Over hill, down into a valley; past tracks of trees and then they raced past a cornfield, and another—and then she realized with a start that they had run to Wusamequin's village, which they had quitted to come here. The wigwams stood empty. The fire ring carried ash.

The demon lurched into a very long wigwam, at least twice as big as any she had seen, and shaped in a U. Moving as one, Isabella and Wusamequin followed it in.

Roaring, the demon shambled toward a figure at the other end of the wigwam. It was an Englishman at the other end of the wigwam, and she knew him. It was Major Samuel Whyte. He was holding a small pair of moccasins and gazing all around, calling, "Miss Stevens?"

The monster swiped at Major Whyte's head but its claw passed through as if it—or Major Whyte—were a ghost. Major Whyte was oblivious to all of it. He continued to examine the moccasins, then moved to a cradle board and picked it up.

The creature threw itself at Major Whyte. Isabella screamed, "Samuel! Have a care!"

Wusamequin gave her a look, planted his feet on the earth, and expertly grabbed an arrow from the quiver over his shoulder. As rapidly as any man with a flintlock, he notched it against his bow and took aim.

*He means to shoot Major Whyte, not the demon!* She didn't know how she knew that, but she did. As surely as she stood there, Wusamequin meant to kill the Englishman.

Isabella shouted, "No!" and rammed Wusamequin; she ran forward with her spear, lodging it hard in the demon's side.

The monster reared back its head and began to shriek as blood gushed from its side. Isabella pushed hard on the spear, and the monster grabbed at her, its clawtips mere inches from her face.

Wusamequin let fly his arrow. It lodged in the demon's neck; as the creature staggered and bellowed in fury, he raced forward, wrapping his hands around hers, shouting, "Mahwah, away!"

She shook her head. Together they forced the creature against the wall, Isabella shrieking in fear but not retreating; and they drove the spear through the creature, pinning it to the wall. Blood bathed the side of the building. Her hands and his were wet with it. Smears covered her dress.

The demon screamed and bellowed, and then was still.

It was dead.

Panting and triumphant, Isabella and Wusamequin threw their arms around each other. He pressed his lips against her, holding her. Her body sang. She held him tight, held him as if to let him go would be to die . . .

"*Wusamequin, nia ktachwahnen,*" she said in her mind, and in her soul.

He responded, ardently. Then suddenly he broke away from her. Stepping backward, he pulled the scalping knife from his waist, pivoted on his heel, and started after Major Whyte.

"No!" Isabella cried. Then the baby magically appeared in Isabella's arms. It was howling, drowning out Isabella's screams.

"No!"

But as Wusamequin raised his knife and prepared to bring it down on the major, who still didn't know either of them were there, the wigwam disappeared. Wusamequin and Major Whyte vanished, and Isabella was back in the chamber, holding nothing in her arms.

She opened her eyes. The room was softly glowing. There was no blood on her hands or her dress. She panted and smoothed back her hair. Wiped perspiration off her brow. Her hands were trembling.

Curled on her grass bed, Afraid-of-Everything raised his head, watching her.

*Did I dream it?* she wondered. *Was he going to kill Major Whyte?*

She slipped on her moccasins and hurried out of the chamber, into the pitch-black tunnel. The wolf padded after her, then caught up and trotted beside her.

At once the torches appeared, lighting their way.

She saw the turn she had missed before, the one that led to the side egress. She took it, rushing along the smaller passageway, and was greeted by gauzy pink sunlight. The new day had dawned . . . and Wusamequin had not returned to the chamber.

Then a woman appeared to her right, trudging down the incline, probably from the entrance to the cavern. It was Wabun-Anung, with snowshoes strapped to her moccasins. Odina and Keshkecho were with her, each carrying a basket on her hip, each also wearing snowshoes.

Afraid-of-Everything growled softly, but when the women hailed Isabella and indicated that she should join them, he slunk forward. She moved with him.

Wabun-Anung handed her basket to Isabella and spoke to her in her native tongue. Then she rattled off a few words to Odina and Keshkecho, who nodded seriously. Wabun-Anung swept past, apparently heading for the main entrance to the cavern.

Isabella understood that she was to go with the two women. She was filled with dread, but Wabun-Anung had ordered it, and she knew she must obey.

They headed for the thick copse of trees where she had seen them emerge yesterday. The snow was dry and powdery, and difficult to walk in. She sank up to her hips. The two Indian women laughed and quickened their pace.

By the time she had caught up with them, they had moved through trees to a vast frozen lake. They were taking off their snowshoes; as she watched them, her gaze traveled to a man-sized hole that had been cut in the ice. They were going to go ice fishing.

Soon they stood in their moccasins. Odina stepped gingerly on the ice, then seemed to think better of it. She waved at Isabella to go first.

Isabella had no recourse but to obey. She walked over the berm of snow and planted her right foot on the frozen water. The cold penetrated her moccasin; she was unsteady from lack of sleep and the ice was slippery. Moreover, she was not wrapped in a fur, as the two other women were.

She began to shiver hard as she minced forward. She knew they were watching her; she could imagine one or both of them rushing forward with a scalping knife, eager to plant it into her back.

Then she reached the hole, set down her basket, and stood beside it, seething with resentment as Odina and Keshkecho sauntered over. Chatting to each other, they pulled coils of what appeared to be fishing lines from their baskets. Each had one; a bone-colored hook was attached to one end. Isabella looked into her own basket, but there was no line. Perhaps Wabun-Anung hadn't planned to stay and fish.

From Odina's basket they also took two pieces of raw fish and baited the hooks with them. Then they lowered the lines into the hole.

Keshkecho's basket also contained a nice bear rug, which she unfolded and laid out on the ice. She and Odina sat down, making no offer to Isabella to join them. She stood on the frozen ice, dizzy with cold, her teeth chattering. Odina pointed at Isabella's mouth and the two laughed heartily.

Mere minutes had passed, but the bone-deep cold was taking its toll. Isabella began to falter, her knees buckling. She held onto Afraid-of-Everything to catch her balance. The wolf leaned against her, supporting her, and giving her as much warmth as he could.

Then Odina gave a happy cry. She jerked on her line, and nodded eagerly at Keshkecho. She had a bite.

"Mahwah," she commanded, pointing imperiously at the line.

Isabella could barely move. She said in English, "I'm freezing. I can't."

Odina scowled at her and pointed again. Then Keshkecho rose, glided over to Isabella, and cuffed her hard on the ear. The blow staggered her.

Afraid-of-Everything growled and bared his teeth.

"No," Isabella rasped, more afraid for the wolf than of the bullying woman. Her ear was ringing. She swayed, and Keshkecho made a fist to hit her again. Isabella moved forward, Afraid-of-Everything shadowing her, protectively moving between her and her tormenter. Keshkecho dropped slightly behind, showing her fist.

Isabella leaned over the hole. Black water greeted her gaze. She could see nothing; she looked at Odina to trace where the fishing line went into the hole, then bent over to pluck it above the water line.

A wave of vertigo hit her. She wobbled back,

forth, back . . .

With a soft shout of protest, she tumbled into the hole, and into the freezing cold water below.

The frigid black water seized her at once. She began to sink as a stinging paralysis numbed her from head to toe. She was so cold she couldn't move; she could barely think. She knew she must not open her mouth, but the pressure to do so was terrible. She had not taken a breath when she'd fallen in, and she was desperate for air.

As she fell through the water, she thought she could hear laughter, but she knew that was impossible.

*They are killing me,* she thought, as she realized that neither of the woman had jumped in after her. *Afraid-of-Everything, get Wusamequin!*

Wusamequin had left the happy mother with her infant daughter. She did not know that without the help of the white skin woman she had insulted, the baby would be dead.

Wusamequin was both elated and very puzzled.

*With Mahwah's help, I used magic to shroud the village from sight. Oneko has confirmed that his envoys could not see any sign of us when they returned this morning from scouting for les Français. We did that together, guiding the stars last night.*

*With her help, I healed the baby. And I found the British soldier who escaped our war party.*

*Together we are more powerful than I am alone. My*

*medicine begins to approach the prowess of my father's—but only by joining with a white skin woman. How can that be?*

He didn't mention any of that now as he sat with Oneko and Sasious in Oneko's tent, telling them how he had seen Major Whyte in a vision, in the long-house of their village.

All three men were alarmed. Oneko said to Wusamequin, "We must send warriors at once to capture this man."

"Agreed," Sasious said. He rose. "I'll go with the warriors. We will return with him in three days."

That made sense to Wusamequin. Warriors could travel at least twice as fast as the village, and it had taken three days to reach the falls.

"Leave warriors here with us as well, in case the Yangees come," Oneko ordered. He turned to Wusamequin and added, "I have faith in the magical veils you placed around our encampment. But we must take all the care we can."

"Agreed," said Wusamequin. Then he turned to Sasious and said, "If you will assemble the warriors, I'll get pollen and sacred ash to anoint them for strength and speed."

"Agreed," said Sasious.

Both men rose. Oneko said, "I sense in my heart that this Yangee has been brought to you in your vision for your final vengeance."

Wusamequin smiled. "My heart soars, Oneko. The spirits are kind."

He left the tent first, refusing to yield to Sasious, who had to stand back and allow it. It was foolish to insult Sasious, however mildly, but he wasn't quite able to restrain himself.

Then as he began to walk briskly toward the little tunnel that led to the chamber he shared with Mahwah, Afraid-of-Everything bounded toward him, barking in the manner he had been taught to signal the presence of danger.

Wusamequin ran toward him and knelt on one knee.

"My brother, what's wrong?" Wusamequin demanded.

Afraid-of-Everything whined and gazed at him. Wusamequin stared into his eyes. He felt himself falling forward, falling . . .

He had an intense, detailed image; he saw it clearly, as if he were there.

*Mahwah, sinking in the icy dark water . . .*

Wusamequin leaped to his feet and raced out the main entrance of the cavern.

*He swam to her. She was cold and lifeless but he jumped in and swam to the bottom of the river, searching for her. Her spirit was working to push off the coil of her body and he swam toward it, holding it by the shoulders, and begging it to go back inside.*

*He carried her to the chamber and he danced for her life. He chanted and begged and sang.*

*He knelt beside her, wrapping her first in cold leather,*

*and then in warm fabric. The Makiawisug knelt with him, weeping. They blew warm breath on her.*

*All this Mahwah saw as she floated above her body, bathed in a brilliant yellow light. Then he shook his rattles and threw back his head and shouted her name, her Christian name:*

"Isabella!"

When Mahwah opened her eyes, Wusamequin knelt beside her, wrapped in a fur that revealed his bare shoulders and forearms. With a sharp intake of breath, he silently grabbed up both her hands in his and kissed her fingertips, one by one. His lips were warm; she felt a glowing energy seeping into her near-frozen flesh.

His eyes shining, his features gentle, he placed her hands on the sides of his face and held them there, warming them even more. They remained that way together; as her chest rose and fell, his did as well.

Then he gathered her in his arms and kissed her forehead, her nose, her temples. His mouth was on hers.

She felt herself coming back to life. She began to shiver violently from the crown of her head to her heels; the pain was like a series of severe blows all over her body.

Wusamequin threw off the fur. She saw his coppery, smooth shoulders and the twin bear tattoos on his chest as he lay down beside her on the fragrant grass bed. He pressed the length of his body against hers. His heat began to melt away the cold. She clung to him, and he to her.

Her four little friends held each other, weeping with joy that she was still with them.

"Do not die, Isabella," Wusamequin whispered. "Do not die."

She burrowed against his warmth, her frozen lips cracking as she replied, "I am called in the manner of Mahwah."

# ❖ Chapter Fifteen ❖

Wusamequin lay with Mahwah in the chamber for what seemed like days. He conjured hot food and drink. He wiped her forehead, chest, and limbs with an unguent he mixed in a stone bowl, which filled the chamber with aromatic steam. It brought her more heat. He rubbed it on her body, then on his own chest and thighs, and enfolded her in his arms.

Mahwah wondered if Odina and Keshkecho had been punished for allowing her to almost drown, but she sincerely doubted that. And Wabun-Anung was no doubt impatient to get her slave back to work. She didn't ask Wusamequin about these things, and he didn't tell her.

There were occasions when he would leave her alone, with stern admonitions not to leave the chamber. She obeyed; she had learned her lesson. Afraid-of-Everything stood guard, and the four fairy people, too.

On one occasion when he returned, his face was clouded with worry, and he didn't smile when he first saw her, as he normally did.

"Aquai," she ventured. She picked up a clay bowl of hot tea, which she had learned to brew from a cache of dried herbs that he had brought into the chamber. *"Menackh."*

*"Wneeweh. Wunneet,"* he said, taking a sip. Then he sighed and crossed his ankles, sinking to the ground.

He took her hand in his, and it seemed natural and right. His face was troubled. "Mahwah. War comes, for the People and the Yangees. Big war. Bad war."

She swallowed. "War? My father? Have you heard anything? The fort? Fort William Henry?"

He turned her hand over and traced the lines in her palm. She watched, wondering if he could read her destiny there.

"The People cannot go back to the village," he told her. "The corn dies. The squash dies. The People die."

They were not going to be able to harvest their crops. She wondered if the freakish early snow had already ruined them.

"I'm sorry," she murmured. Then she peered up at him through her lashes. "But perhaps there is a way to make peace. My people are not warlike. They—"

"Your words are crooked." His tone was harsh. His eyes flashed. "Your people love war. Your people war on my people."

"No," she cut in. "That's not true. The French are like that. But the English people only wish to share this land with your people. We are only trying to protect ourselves from hostile Indians and the French. We have no wish to war on you."

He swirled his teacup and gazed into it; then cocked his head and studied her, as if trying to make a decision. Suddenly she was unaccountably nervous.

"Wusamequin? What hurts your heart?" Her voice was soft and tentative as she touched first her own heart with the flat of her left hand, and then his. "My heart hurts when your heart hurts."

She expected him to smile at that, but he did not. Instead he turned to the wall and flung his hand toward it. Then he crossed his arms over his chest.

"See," he announced. "The Yangees and their war."

When an image formed on the wall, she rose and walked toward it. She was used to the magic now, accustomed to the fact that Wusamequin wielded powerful medicine.

She saw before her the village they had abandoned. It was autumn, as it was now, brilliant carpets of leaves rushing along the ground as a dozen children in warm leather jerkins and leggings capered and laughed. Puppies yipped at their heels, and one little wolf cub. By his markings she realized it was Afraid-of-Everything, and she smiled faintly at his round baby-shape head and gangling paws.

Smoke rose from the wigwams. Passenger pigeons flew overhead. A woman stepped out of a hut, cupping her hands around her mouth. One of the children veered off from the others and raced toward her, dancing like a fawn.

Wusamequin waved his hand again, and the image changed. Now Isabella viewed the inside of a wigwam. A dainty young Indian woman sat by the fire with a baby in her arms. Her dress was brilliantly decorated with bears similar to the tattoos on Wusamequin's chest. Her hair hung down in glossy braids, and a braided headband glittered with bear-print designs. Her brown eyes were half-closed and she was smiling dreamily as she took one of her braids and tickled the babe's face. The baby sneezed, and the woman giggled. She sang in a high, lilting voice with a small but pleasingly full mouth. The baby cooed contentedly in reply.

Then the sound stopped. The image went silent.

Surprised, Mahwah glanced over at Wusamequin, who was staring straight ahead, as if he had forgotten she was there.

"Is this . . ." Mahwah swallowed hard without taking her gaze off the fetching tableau of mother and child. "Is this your family?"

He did not reply, but the veins stood out in his forehead and his neck. He was straining against powerful emotions.

Mahwah wasn't sure she wanted to see more.

Light flared around her, a nimbus of it like the figures painted on the rocks of the chamber. In the next instant, she was standing in the wigwam with the dainty woman, who did not realize she was there. Mahwah understood. It was the same as when they had seen Major Whyte; she was like a ghost.

Suddenly the woman jerked and widened her eyes. She grabbed the baby against her chest and ran to the door of the wigwam. Isabella followed.

A British soldier was chasing the children, and

the little ones were panicking. His tricorne was askew and his face was dirty as he tore after them, laughing hard.

In his right hand, he carried a musket.

The little ones were crying; their mouths gaped open as if they were screaming in terror. The woman gestured toward them, urging them toward the wigwam, but they ran.

Then one little girl fell, and the British soldier behind her stopped, raised his musket, and took aim.

The woman tore out of the wigwam and ran toward the soldier. She bowed her body protectively around her infant, waving her hands and shouting words Mahwah could not hear.

By that time, other women were emerging from their wigwams. Some were racing from the cornfields.

The soldier with the musket shifted it from the little girl to the woman in the bear-print dress. He had an ugly face, pocked and scarred, and it was demonic as he took aim and positioned his finger on the trigger.

Mahwah's warning scream was soundless.

He fired.

The woman was thrown off her feet.

The baby flew into the air. Mahwah tried to catch it, but she could not; she could only watch helplessly as the baby landed in a pile of leaves.

Blood blossomed on the front of the Indian woman's leather dress. She reached out a hand toward the baby and began to crawl toward it, her face twisted with agony. Closer, closer she crawled ...

A second soldier charged at her, grabbing her under the arm and dragging her along the ground as she strained toward the baby. Her moccasins kicked up leaves, obscuring Mahwah's view as she tried to reach the baby. Mahwah batted at the colors, crying and weeping, in the hideous silence.

A third soldier bounded over to the pile of leaves. He hefted the baby under his arm and headed out of the village with the others. Old men and more women were rushing out of the wigwams with tomahawks and knives, chasing after the intruders.

Then Wusamequin flew into Mahwah's field of vision, wet with sweat and dressed only in a loincloth. His hair was slicked back, and he carried a tomahawk. His face was a rictus of terror. Mahwah had seen such tremendous fear only once before in her life: on the face of her mother, when she had been told they must remain in the Colonies because of the war.

He ran after the men dragging his wife and child out of their village, his tomahawk at the ready. But one of the British soldiers wheeled around and butted Wusamequin hard in the face with the barrel of his musket.

"No!" Mahwah cried, but her voice was silent.

Wusamequin collapsed face first into the leaves as the Englishman turned his musket around. The bayonet had been fixed; he shoved the sharp point under Wusamequin's skull, then dragged it hard down Wusamequin's spine. A huge, deep gash erupted, bleeding profusely.

Wusamequin lay unmoving.

More British descended on the village, laughing, discharging their weapons in the air, at the village pets. Mahwah was only slightly aware of them as she knelt beside Wusamequin and reached out her hand to touch his wound.

Her hand went right through his body.

"I can't bear this. Don't make me see this!" she pleaded, her words still unheard. Tears slid down her face.

In a trice she was back in the chamber. She was so sickened by what she had seen that she wrapped her arms around herself, rooted to the spot.

She looked down at her fair white skin. In that moment, she wished she could rip it from her arms. She hated that she was English. She hated all English.

Her sobs came hard. She wanted him to comfort her but she couldn't stand herself, couldn't stop seeing what she had seen.

He didn't speak. Didn't touch her. She keened in her misery, sick to the depths of her soul.

Then she thought of him.

He was the one whose wife and child had been murdered. He was the one who had grieved and mourned their untimely deaths. No matter that she was English. He had opened his heart to her.

She should be the one to offer comfort, not he.

"I . . . am . . . sorry," she managed, her voice raw and hoarse. She looked up at him. "I . . ."

As she fumbled for speech, a single tear formed at the corner of his eye. It hovered there, and she saw lines of despair and grief in his face; she saw his lips trembling. He was as taut as a bow.

The tear spilled from his eye and ran down his cheek.

"Oh," she whispered.

She reached up her finger and touched the tear. He grabbed her finger, held it, and for a moment she was afraid that she had done something unforgivable, just as her countrymen had.

Then he placed his left hand over the left bear tattoo on his chest. She heard a distant growl, from somewhere very, very far away; then he brought his hand away from his chest and opened his palm.

Resting in his palm was a shiny black figurine of a bear, which resembled in every way his tattoo. A glance at his chest revealed that the tattoo had disappeared.

He touched her tear-laden finger against the figurine. Then he pressed his fingertip into the streak of tears on her own face, and touched that to the bear as well.

He took her left hand, lacing his fingers between his, and began to chant. The melody thrummed in her soul. From her heart to fingertips, she joined the chant.

The Makiawisug clung to his moccasins, weeping. Titania knelt and laid her head on the colorful quill bear design.

Their hands still laced, he walked her to his side

of the chamber and sat her down on the grass bed. He had to assist her; she was so shaky she couldn't manage it herself. The terrible images she had seen kept replaying in her mind.

Numb, she watched as he moved the grass from the lower portion of the bed and extracted a large woven basket. He opened the lid and pulled out a pair of tiny moccasins. His large hands dwarfed them.

He lowered his head over them and chanted. Then he handed them to her. She cradled them as if they were the most precious and fragile things on the earth. There was only one thing more precious, more fragile:

The father of the child whose moccasins these were.

His voice rose and fell, as he took out a small leather bag threaded through with a leather thong. From the basket he also took dried tobacco, and many, many herbs, and put them into the bag. Next he placed the hoof of a deer, a white eagle's feather, a yellow feather . . . and, taking them from her, the tiny moccasins. Lastly, he placed the bear figurine inside the bag and drew the thong, closing the bag.

He moved back on his heels and rose, still chanting. He held the bag out and faced the vine curtain that separated their two halves of the chamber. Then he made a quarter turn, and a third, and a fourth. He raised the bag toward the ceiling, then toward the floor.

A warm glow filled the chamber, swirling in a

golden haze. Mahwah heard a young woman's sweet voice, and a baby's shy and happy laughter. The glow faded; then the bag took on the luster of gold, then became a plain leather pouch once more.

Wusamequin held it out to her.

"Isabella," he said, "keep. Strong medicine." He cleared his throat and touched his heart. "Wusamequin." He pointed at the bag. "Wusamequin's spirit lives there. Keep always. The bag keeps Mahwah safe."

He reached forward and took the bag from her, tying it by the thong to the belt at her waist. He touched it. "Odina and Keshkecho make war on Isabella. Your heart knows this."

"I understand. It is for protection," she said. She lowered her head. "Thank you." She looked back up at him and added, "I am called in the manner of Mahwah now." It was the second time she had reminded him.

He said nothing, only looked very sad.

Rapid footfalls sounded outside the chamber. Wusamequin held out a hand to indicate that she should stay where she was. She nodded. He got up and parted the curtain of flowers.

A man's voice greeted him, speaking in an excited tone. Wusamequin's voice rose as well. She heard the joy in it and wondered what was going on.

He poked his head through the vines and said, "Mahwah, stay."

Then he left.

She wondered what was going on, but she knew that this time, she shouldn't go investigating on her own. She sat touching the pouch. The Makiawisug gathered in her lap, Titania still very low from witnessing what they had seen.

She brewed tea, and drank it, offering some to her little friends. She dozed.

Wusamequin did not return.

"I wish I knew what was happening," she said aloud.

Instantly, an image gleamed upon the wall.

She gasped.

Major Samuel Whyte lay outside in the snow, bloodied and beaten. Six braves stood heavily armed with tomahawks and scalping knives.

A rope around his neck half-choked him; it was attached to a stake, around which kindling had been arranged. They were going to scalp him and burn him!

Then she saw Wusamequin walking toward Major Whyte with his knife in his hand. Oneko stood to one side with his arms folded, watching with a grim smile.

"No, no!" Mahwah cried. "No!"

The pouch at her side shifted as if something were alive inside it. She gasped and lifted her arms away from it, frightened. She ran into the tunnel; the torches lighted. She turned the corner to go out the side entrance and—

—Wusamequin was there, in the tunnel.

She collided with him, ramming hard against his

chest. He grabbed her as if he had fully expected to see her there, and wrapped his hand around her forearm as he began to walk her back toward the chamber.

"Oh, no, please. Please, don't," she said frantically, trying to free herself. "He's not the one who did it. Don't!"

He looked at her as if he didn't know her. As they entered the chamber, he said, "Yangee."

"But I am Yangee," she said. "You spared me."

"Yangee *soldier*," he corrected. He added, "His spirit is weak."

"Is he sick?" she asked. At his look, she put both her hands around his neck and raised herself on tiptoe, studying his face. "Please, please tell me. Is there plague at the fort? My father, is my father all right?"

He said, "I do not know."

"But can you see? Can you make medicine to show me the fort?" she begged. Her mind was racing. "Wusamequin, you cannot kill that man!"

"Wusamequin can," he retorted, removing her hands from around his neck and moving her away from himself. "And Wusamequin will."

# ❧ Chapter Sixteen ❧

The single tear that Wusamequin had shed had weakened him.

His spirit had been misled; he had begun to open his heart to the captive Yangee. The magic they created together was more powerful than anything he had ever done alone. But he had forgotten one thing: that she was a white skin, and all white skins were his enemy.

Now, as he led Isabella Stevens outside to speak to Whyte, he cursed himself for the tear. Using that essence of his full, deep self, he had put his spirit inside the bear fetish, in order to protect her. Now he no longer belonged solely to himself. But in doing so, he had divided his loyalties and his obligations between the People and her. It was a foolish and selfish mistake.

Isabella pulled her fur wrap around herself, and he walked her to the forlorn hollow in the outcropping of the cliff. There the prisoner lay huddled on a bearskin, which was more than he deserved. Sasious's braves had done it, to show Wusamequin that they valued the trophy they were presenting to him. Ninigret was there, and chubby Tashtassuck, and

Wematin. Men who valued him, esteemed him.

"Samuel!" Isabella cried, racing to the man kneeling beside him.

"You're alive!" the Yangee soldier said hoarsely as he gazed up at her.

His face was pasty, his lips chapped. With a growing sense of alarm, Wusamequin studied the changes in him since he had last seen him. The man's spirit had been thoroughly invaded.

Isabella touched his forehead. Her eyes widened as she moved her hand to the side of his face. Wusamequin couldn't stand to see him treated with such concern. He crossed his arms over his chest and averted his gaze.

*I have been a weak fool,* he told himself. *I shall be one no longer.*

In a rush of both fear for him and joy to see him, Mahwah wrapped her arms around Samuel Whyte. He began to whisper; she put her ear to his mouth as he croaked out more words.

"I didn't desert you that day," he murmured. "You must know that. I knew they would butcher all the men. My single thought was to survive, so that I could go to the fort and tell them what I had seen. To mount a rescue party and come back for you."

"Thank you." She took off her fur robe and draped it around his shoulders. "What about my father?" she asked.

"Living, but quite ill," Whyte confessed. "He has been so afraid for you that he hasn't been able to rest.

He watches night and day for the courier dispatches, to see if there is any sign of you." He hesitated.

"I pray you, be honest with me," she entreated.

"Well, then." He sighed as if to prepare himself for words that would cost him dearly. "I fear that he may be dying." His cough was like a death rattle, and icy fear skittered up her spine. "As I am. You must get away from me, Isabella. I have the pestilence."

"Ah, no!"

"We lost the medicine that day. Another shipment was sent, but it may have been too late to be of any use." He stared at her. "I hardly recognized you, in those heathen clothes and your hair in those plaits. You must have been enslaved. Have they mistreated you?"

"At first," she conceded. "I'm not well liked."

"It may be a blessing that they took you that day." He sighed. His voice was tired. "So many have died. The fort is like a tomb." He coughed again, hard, and spit up more blood.

Alarmed, she raised her eyes to Wusamequin, and said, "Wusamequin, I beg of you. Let us make medicine for him." She held out her left hand, the one they held together when they made magic. "Please."

Oneko turned to Wusamequin and said, "What is she saying?"

"She wishes me to heal the Yangee." Wusamequin's voice shook from the insult.

Oneko nodded, as if his answer had confirmed his suspicions. Sasious spat in the snow. "Best we burn her with him."

Wusamequin did not reach out his medicine hand to her. He said to her in English, "My wife. My son. The Yangees sent them to the Land Beyond. Now it is fourteen moons, and they walk the Road of Stars. This one must die. It is my Way."

"No, don't say that," she pleaded. "I saw. It was horrible. But his death will not help."

"The Yangee deaths did help. My spirit was freed. My medicine was strong again."

"Oh, God, oh, dear God!" Isabella cried. "You cannot mean that. You don't mean that! Please, at least let him have some water. He's burning up with fever." She touched the man's forehead and held him against her breast.

Oneko asked in their language, "Is he her husband?"

It had never dawned on Wusamequin to ask her if she was married. Now, as he observed the pains she was taking with the man, his heart chilled.

"Isabella," he said in English, "Whyte shares your wigwam?"

"No." The surprise on her face brought Wusamequin relief.

As Mahwah held the sick major, Whyte coughed hard, and then he said, "I wish that were true, Isabella. I wish we could have married." He coughed again, harder, so hard that blood trickled from the side of his mouth.

"Samuel . . ."

"Ah. My name." His eyes took on a strange light. "An angel speaks it before I die."

"No! You shall not die!" she shouted. "Do you hear me?"

"I am dying." His expression grew soft. "I have searched for you everywhere. Others had accompanied me, but there has been so much illness . . ."

"It is all right," she assured him.

He went on, "It was as if the village had been under a spell. I must have ridden past it a dozen times before I saw it."

He moved his glance from her to Sasious. "It was deserted, and I knew they had taken you somewhere else. I was at a loss. And then they attacked me in the village, as if they knew I was there. They captured me, and brought me here."

He smiled weakly at her and added, "It is a miracle that I have found you."

"No, it was my doing," she confessed, awash in guilt. "I didn't mean to lead them to you. I didn't know."

"No matter." His smile was weak, but it was there. "I have a signed letter of safe passage for you," he murmured. "The French should honor it. And a map from the village to the fort. Both are folded very tiny."

Surreptitiously she felt in his uniform pocket for the documents. She found a wad of thick paper and cupped it. His body shielded her actions as she forced open Wusamequin's medicine bag with her fingertips and dropped the paper inside.

"It's done," she whispered.

He exhaled and slurred, "Then I've done my duty."

As he slumped, his eyes drooping, she gently shook his shoulders. "Oh, Samuel, don't die. Please don't die!"

He didn't respond. His weight burdensome against her chest, she clasped her hands together as best she could, holding them out to Wusamequin. "Please, oh, please, help me heal him!"

"Look how she begs, like a dog," Sasious sneered. "So emotional and out of control. I was a fool to want her in my wigwam."

"My wife agrees," Oneko said. "She's weak in all respects. She's not good for much."

"We will burn him," Wusamequin told her in English. There was no response from Whyte.

"You cannot mean that!" She looked frantic. "You cannot!"

He raised a hand and took a step toward her, thinking to strike her for her insolence. "You do not speak so!" he shouted. "You are my slave!"

"I am not!" she shouted back at him. "Search your heart. You know that I am not!" She clung to the limp Yangee. "He is a human being! You are a healer! You must help him!"

"This is an outrage. You should beat her," Sasious observed. His six braves shifted their weight and toyed with their weaponry as they watched the unfolding tableau. It was clear they understood most of what was happening; and that, like him, they couldn't believe that Wusamequin was hesitating to stake his claim on the Yangee's hair because of the white skin squaw. And arguing about it with her, no less.

Oneko's attention shifted from Isabella to Wusamequin, obviously waiting for the shaman to do something.

Wusamequin's weak heart watched her grief. It watched her tears. It understood that if he burned the Yangee, her own heart would be strong against him for the rest of her life.

But he had made a vow.

He sensed Oneko's dismay, and on Sasious's part at least, his disgust. The weakness of the People's third leader, on display for all to see, mortified them.

*I must speak to Great Bear*, he thought. *I need his counsel.* But there was no time.

"Isabella," he began, his voice flat. Then he saw the face of the Yangee. The man's mouth drooped open. His eyes were open but he was not looking at this world.

The choice had been made for Wusamequin. The burden had been lifted from his shoulders.

"The Yangee is dead," he said in the language to Oneko and Sasious.

Oneko's brows raised. He cocked his head, peering at the Yangee, and nodded. "So he is. Evil spirits have taken him."

"Good riddance," Sasious muttered, spitting in the snow.

Isabella was watching them. Then she bent her arm and allowed the Yangee's head to loll into the crook of her arm.

When she saw his open eyes, she inhaled sharply and whispered, "No." She wailed like a wolf. "No! Oh, God, please no!"

Afraid-of-Everything, who had trotted up beside Wusamequin, sat back on his haunches and lifted his head to the sky. He joined his voice with hers, and the two howled in chorus.

"What a display," Sasious said above the cacophony.

"Does this white woman rule you now?" Oneko asked Wusamequin.

Wusamequin took one step toward Isabella, and she clutched the dead man to her.

"Don't touch him, don't you touch him!" she cried. "Leave him alone!"

He put his hand around her upper arm and half-lifted, half-dragged her to her feet. She fought to keep hold of the corpse, but she could not. It was too heavy.

Wordlessly, he marched her past the eight men. Over his shoulder, he said to Oneko and Sasious, "I'll return. Let me take his hair before you get rid of him."

"Of course," Sasious replied. The braves were smiling, delighted that the shaman would claim his gift.

Mahwah was frantic as he herded her back to the chamber. Afraid-of-Everything had stopped howling, but he was whimpering, aware that something was seriously amiss between Mahwah and his beloved Wusamequin.

He threw her onto her bed. The heads of the four Makiawisug popped from the grass and the little people darted out of the way.

"I will take his hair, and I will put it on my scalp pole!" he shouted at her. "Stay here, Isabella. If you do not . . ." He made a fist and showed it to her.

"You're a coward, to threaten a woman!" she screamed. "I hate you!"

"Silence!" he thundered at her.

Then he turned his back on her and stomped away.

The Makiawisug climbed onto her, patting her face and stroking her forehead. Her mind raced. She said to them in English, "I cannot bear this! My father is ill. I must go. I must leave. Now."

They looked up at her. She sat up carefully, allowing them to slide into her palms. Then she set them down, trying to formulate a plan as she ran her shaking fingers over the crown of her head.

"How can I escape?" she asked them.

She did not wait for a reply as she tore apart the room, opening baskets and peeking in clay bowls and gourds. She found some dried fruit and cornmeal, a large cache of dried meat, and herbs for tea. Soon she had a small pile; she searched some more, then found a small piece of leather in which to bundle it up.

She would need a fur to wrap in. If only she had her own snowshoes . . .

Titania looked from the bundle to Isabella and back again. Then she held up a hand as if to stop her. Isabella shook her head. "I have to go," she said gently. "My father is ill. There is . . . there's no place for me here." She picked up the bundle. "I shall miss you, Titania. You have all been so kind to me."

The little fairy queen cupped her hands around her mouth and turned toward the curtain of flowering vines. The vines began to shake and undulate. Then more tiny Makiawisug faces popped from behind the lush blossoms. Mahwah counted two, three . . . six . . . at least a dozen.

The fairies grinned at her and waved. Then they began jumping onto the flowers, their weight separating the blossoms from the vines. As soon as a flower would break from its stalk, they would set to working on plucking another. Soon a shower of blossoms was dropping onto Wusamequin's bed.

"This is so sweet," Mahwah told them. "But I haven't time . . ."

Then Titania grasped the nearest petal and gestured for Mahwah to take it. Her tiny face was wild with urgency.

"What?" Mahwah asked.

Titania said, "*Tpochgo. Pachkenum.*" She pointed to Mahwah's hands and pretended to crush the flower between her palms.

Mahwah complied, picking up the flower and crushing the petals as Titania showed her. From its pale yellow juice, an intoxicating fragrance filled the room.

And Mahwah's fingertips disappeared!

"What?" she cried. She held up the flower. "This is magic? This can make me disappear?"

She picked up another flower and squeezed it into her palm. Where the liquid touched, that part of her flesh vanished as well.

"Oh, thank you!" she cried.

At Titania's urging, she lay on her side on Wusamequin's bed and squeezed the blossoms into a clay bowl that Oberon and Puck dragged over to her. The four-and-twenty Makiawisug dipped the petals in the liquid and began to rub it over her clothes and exposed skin. They even rubbed it into her hair and onto her bundle of food.

"Hurry, hurry," she begged, helping as best she could. She wiped the liquid on her face. Her heart was skipping beats; she was crazed with fear that Wusamequin would come back before they were finished.

At last they were done. Puck and Cobweb helped Isabella fill her invisible bundle with more blossoms. She raced into the hall and down the tunnel. She knew she musn't go out the side way; Wusamequin and the other men were out there. He might not see her, but it was likely that he could magically sense her presence.

She glanced down at her hands, and saw nothing.

She had no idea how long the magic lasted, but she knew she must seize the moment. Another would not come.

So she ran down the corridor to the entrance into the main cavern. Taking a deep breath, she emerged, glancing fearfully at the Indian guards posted on either side. Neither reacted.

She hurried through the cavern and out the main entrance, stepping onto the ledge behind the waterfall. She kept well away from the spray, assuming that if any of the flower juice were washed off, that part of her would become visible again.

Though she wanted to run, she moved slowly and carefully along the slimy rocks. Sure enough, once the bottoms of her moccasins absorbed moisture, they were visible.

She left the ledge and clambered up the staircase toward the crest of the cliff. She was breathless with fear.

At the top, she stopped and peered over the ledge.

Something was burning where Samuel Whyte had died. She imagined it was his body. She nodded grimly. It was less likely the People would catch the disease this way. But she knew he would have wanted to be buried properly.

She took a breath and whispered, "Farewell, Wusamequin. Farewell, Afraid-of-Everything." She swallowed down a lump. "Rest in peace, Samuel Whyte."

Then she turned and faced the wilderness. She

had no idea which way to go.

Something tugged on her braid. Then a little voice chattered in her ear.

"Titania!" she cried.

The fairy queen must have crawled into her bundle. She was invisible.

As were the other Makiawisug who yanked on her braids. She felt around for them and counted a total of four; her dear quartet. They had come with her.

"*Wneeweh*," she said feelingly. Then she tried to explain where they needed to go. If they could lead her to the village, she could try to use the map from there. Unless it, too, had become invisible.

But when she brought it from her medicine bag, she could still see it. She unfolded it, alarmed to see that the edges had soaked in some of the liquid and become invisible. But the body of the map was visible. There were the mountains they had traveled over, and there a stream. And there was a good sketch of Fort William Henry as well.

Titania and the others chattered excitedly.

Mahwah dared to hope. "Do you know how to get to the fort?"

Of course they didn't understand, but their excited chatter did not fade.

She sent a prayer to the heavens, and then she set out.

The Makiawisug found the path the tribe had traveled from the village to the falls, and that made it easier to cover territory. But it was very cold, and she didn't know what she would do when night fell and it grew colder still.

As the sun dipped, she began to panic. She thought of her warm chamber, and the delicious food Wusamequin would prepare. The hot tea she would brew. The magic they could now conjure . . . together.

She shivered hard. Her little friends burrowed inside her fur, lending her a tiny bit of warmth.

An owl hooted. Creatures rustled in the underbrush on either side of the path as protective shadows lengthened around them.

Then she heard the distant, steady pounding of horse hooves along the ground, and she darted from the path into the brush. She began to tremble. God only knew what they would do to her if they caught her trying to escape.

As she watched through the gloom, Dulcie, her little mare, cantered to a halt. The sidesaddle and double bridle were nowhere to be seen, but a number of thick Indian blankets and furs had been secured across her back. A large basket had been tied to her side as well.

Isabella gingerly approached. The little mare whinnied, standing quite still. She patted the horse and said softly, "It is I, sweet Dulcie. Mahwah." Then she heard herself and said, "Isabella."

But she wasn't Isabella anymore.

She opened the basket and peered inside. There was more dried food, and several clay bowls, and some gourds. Isabella smelled the contents of one of the bowls; sure enough, it was the heat unguent Wusamequin had used on her.

In the bottom of the basket lay a shiny black bear figurine identical to the one in the medicine bag at her waist.

Her eyes brimmed.

"*Wneeweh*, Wusamequin," she said aloud.

She made sure the four Makiawisug were with her. Then she mounted the mare, and began to ride.

# ❖ Chapter Seventeen ❖

The fort.

A miracle to see, and yet . . . here she was.

Though the water had been icy, she had bathed the juice off herself in a nearby stream and unbraided her hair. Then she put some of the heating potion onto her arms and legs to warm herself up.

She could not coax the Makiawisug to come inside the fort with her, and she did not know if they lurked in the forest beyond, or if they had scampered for home.

Despite her attire, the sentries hailed her into the fort. They understood who she was, and one, a young man named Jamie Munsfield, escorted her to the infirmary.

There he was. Her father, her own.

She knelt at the side of his wooden trundle bed in the fort infirmary and grabbed up his hand, kissing it, then leaned forward and showered his face with kisses.

"Poppet," he murmured joyously, raising himself on his elbow. He wore a nightshirt, and he had been much reduced by his illness. "Look at you."

One of the women of the fort had bustled off to

find her something to wear and something to eat. She was cold and hungry, but nothing could have kept her from her father's side.

A chair was brought, and strong tea and a blanket. Sipping the tea, she told him of her life among the Indians, saying only that Wusamequin, the medicine man who had treated his shoulder, had sheltered her and protected her from the wrath of the tribe at large.

"Sometimes white women are brought into the tribe," he ventured. "Either as slaves or wives."

Her face grew hot. She recalled his having used the term "marriage" to describe the untenable situation savage men were said to force upon civilized ladies, and knew that she would never tell him what had passed between her and Wusamequin.

At the thought of him, her heart squeezed painfully.

"I was not a wife," she answered truthfully. "And though told I was a slave, seldom treated as one."

"Should I ever see Wusamequin again, I should like to thank him," her father told her. "He seemed a gentleman among savages." He stirred. "What of Major Whyte? He told us he was off to search for you. For my money, he was escaping the fort, in fear of the sickness."

"Samuel . . . that is, Major Whyte, died of the pestilence," she added, refraining yet again from going into detail.

Her father's face hardened. "He abandoned us to the savages."

"No. He assured me that he did not. He hoped to survive, so that he could rescue us."

"A pretty fiction," her father retorted. "Ah, well, one must not speak ill of the dead. And you are here now, my darling girl." He sniffed the air. "There is a pleasant odor in the room."

"It is special salve. They use it to keep themselves warm," she explained. She reached into her medicine pouch and took out the unguent Wusamequin had packed for her. After rubbing some on her hands, she stroked her father's forehead with it.

"Ah, most efficacious," he said happily.

She placed it back in the pouch and pulled it shut. The infirmary door banged open. Colonel Ramsland, the commander of the fort, strode into the room in his noisy boots. He was a stringy, soldierly type of man, splendid in his uniform, all buttons gleaming, with an ivory-colored wig beneath his tricorne.

Mahwah rose to signal her respect, and swept him a deep curtsey. She must have looked a sight in her Indian costume.

"So it's true," he said jovially. "The young lady is restored to us."

"It's true," she agreed.

"Providence is most kind."

"Indeed, sir."

He gestured for her to sit, which she did. "Forgive me for coming to you just after you're arrived, but I must ask you questions before certain details blessedly fade from your memory."

"Of course, Colonel," she said, the soul of a compliant, well-bred young lady. Inwardly, however, she was most nervous.

He rubbed his hands together. "It's deucedly cold today. What of that snow, eh? The Colonials are frantic about their crops."

He leaned forward. "I trust it snowed where you were being held prisoner."

"Yes, it did," she agreed.

He nodded to himself. "Very good. Where were they then, these fiends? Can you describe their encampment to us? Help us locate it?"

She had prepared herself for this. And she had not known what she would do or say ... until this moment.

*Wusamequin trusted me. He let me go knowing I might lead them back.*

"Sir, alas, I cannot," she lied, her eyes enormous and innocent. "I gave Dulcie her head, and my little mare found her way home. The forest was so dark and frightening ..."

"Were there mountains?" he asked patiently.

"Aye, everywhere." She touched her forehead. "If you don't mind sir, I am sorry, but I have no idea where I was taken."

The man sighed heavily. "As I had feared. One assumes that a young lady brought up in the hustle and bustle of London would find the wilderness unremarkable, save in its endless oppressiveness."

"Quite," Mahwah concurred.

"Well, then I should like to also know how many warriors they had, and how they were armed—"

"Sir, with your permission," Mahwah demurred. "I am freezing and hungry."

"Of course." He swept her a small bow. "My apologies. Doctor, again, my felicitations upon the restoration of your child to you."

"Thank you, sir," Mahwah's father replied, beaming at her. "I am certain it will be easier for her to cooperate once she has had some food and rest."

"Indeed, sir," Mahwah said, curtseying again.

"I look forward to that," Colonel Ramsland said.

As the colonel quitted the infirmary, Maude O'Malloy, the woman who had brought Mahwah her tea, swept back in. She was the wife of one of the Colonial Militia attached to the fort. She had been hired to help with the cooking, and also because she spoke both French and some Iroquois.

"We must change you out of those wet things, Miss Stevens," she said to Mahwah. Then, with a mischievous grin, she reached into the pocket of her apron and produced a letter. "It's Mrs. DeWitt again."

"Ah. How pleasant." Dr. Stevens smiled at Mahwah as he reached for the letter. "She will be delighted to hear of your daring escape."

"Indeed," Isabella said. She was pleased that the two had started up a correspondence.

Mrs. O'Malloy led her out of the room and down a flight of stairs. She said, "We live here."

She pushed open a door. Isabella walked into a plain but rustic sitting room that reminded her somewhat of Albany. Her own home was far grander, but it had been a long month since she had stood in a room with English furniture. There was a painting over the mantel, of the tame, green fields of home.

"I'll bring you hot water," Mrs. O'Malloy told her. "I've laid out a dressing gown on the bed."

"Thank you. You're too kind," Mahwah said, suddenly overcome with the realization that she was back among her own people.

*But if they are my people, why do I feel so tremendously out of place?*

"Not at all. After what you've been through . . . Welcome home, miss." The woman bobbed a curtsey and left Mahwah to her privacy.

As the door shut, Mahwah sank into a chair. She opened the medicine bag at her waist and took out the two bear figurines—the one that had originally been in the bag, and the second one, which Wusamequin had placed in the basket of food. Two large tears spilled down her cheeks; one splashed on the bear in her left hand.

"How are you faring, Wusamequin?" she whispered.

Blossoming like a rose, an image formed on the wall.

It was he.

She saw his profile etched against the setting sun. He was standing in their chamber, and in his hand he held the shredded remnants of her pale green traveling coat.

As she watched, he buried his face in it.

The image faded.

She choked back tears as she put the two bears back into her bag. Then she peeled off her Indian clothing and slipped on the dressing gown.

With her arms around her, shivering with cold and weeping with grief, she leaned back in a chair to wait for the hot water, and she fell asleep.

Oneko joined Wusamequin on the ledge overlooking the waterfall. The two stood in companionable silence.

"In the matter of the horse," Oneko began. "Odina has confessed that she had gone to visit them, and forgot to shut the gate."

Wusamequin gathered his fur wrap around himself as he watched the steam rise off the waterfall. The day was clear and cold. The sky, brittle and sad. He knew Odina wished to gain favor with him with the lie.

"Are we safe here?" Oneko asked him.

Wusamequin thought a moment. "To be safe, perhaps we should move again."

Anchored at the crown of his head, Oneko's feathers fluttered in the breeze. He could count great coup at the council fires of his ancestors. He was lucky.

"I am too old for this," he grumbled. "Before, when we moved, it was to enjoy the gifts of the Mother. For sugaring time among the maple trees. To catch young shad and harvest oysters. Now, we scatter like mice simply to avoid confrontation. Sasious thinks we should attack the fort, especially if the Yangees are weak and sick."

Wusamequin was shocked. "They have more weapons than we shall ever have."

"Our hearts are stronger."

"They can shoot our hearts." Wusamequin looked hard at his leader. "Do Sasious's words walk straight with you?"

"We are warriors," Oneko replied thoughtfully. "All this hiding . . ." He gestured to the encampment. "We're living like rodents. This cannot be the People's Way."

Wusamequin knew this was a terribly important conversation. Oneko had not idly joined him to admire the scenery. He said, "Great Sachem Oneko, the tides have turned. We were a great people, but sickness and war have preyed on us. We must find a way to survive, until the white skins tire of persecuting us and move on to other things. That is our Way in this time."

Oneko raised a brow as he folded his arms over his chest. "Is that what your heart tells you? That the great People of the River should allow this mistreatment?"

Wusamequin felt his elder's sorrow and shame. He felt his own. He wished he could speak other words, but it was his responsibility to be honest, if his words could affect the welfare of the people. And they could.

"Onkeo, my heart tells me that we must do what we can to survive. We cannot attack the fort."

They were both silent for a moment. Then Oneko said, "Following that argument, you should marry Odina. To survive. You need living children in this world so that you can pass on your legacy. You cannot be the last of Miantonomi's seed." He smiled faintly. "Had *I* a chance to put sons in Odina's belly . . . But I'm an old man."

Wusamequin felt weary. "She is a sister to me."

Oneko cut in, "Mahwah is gone."

"She was called in the manner of Isabella," Wusamequin replied. "She was a white skin woman."

"You cherished her," Oneko said bluntly. "Don't deny it. Yet if you had had sons with her, they would not have been sons of the People. Nor sons of the Yangees. They would have been no one's sons. There is no land for them. No refuge from cold and hunger.

"In both places, they would have been outcasts."

Wusamequin thought again of the medicine bag he had given her. He wondered if she understood its significance; she carried his spirit with her. The man who stood before his leader was not a whole man. He had been split in two. Such a man could not love anyone.

Could not make sons with another.

"Your *sister* approaches," Oneko drawled.

Clearly it was no accident when Odina appeared

from behind an outcropping of rock. Oneko and Odina had planned this ambush, and she was dressed for the war dance of the heart. She was wearing a fine leather cape covered with feathers, and her hair gleamed with beads and silver. She was graceful as she moved, despite her snowshoes.

Moving away, Oneko clasped Wusamequin on the shoulder. "Of the women who love you, Odina is most suitable."

Wusamequin silently nodded.

His elder departed just as Odina reached Wusamequin's side. She was radiant. Her skin glowed. She was very young and very pretty.

He continued to stare at her, wishing he could feel for her. But his spirit was not with him.

"Wusamequin?" she asked flirtatiously. "Do you see the care I've taken for you?"

He began to sweat. Heat washed over him like wind. He parted his lips and murmured, "The bag. They are burning the bag."

Then his heart stopped.

He lurched right, left, swaying, and then he fell backward.

Down he soared, headfirst down, down, into the icy cascade as it thundered and crashed around him.

Down, as the water beat and battered him.

Down . . .

*And he sank in the icy, churning waters, his breath knocked out of him. In his heavy clothes, he could not swim.*

*The force of the falls kept him under, and under, and still, his heart did not beat.*

*Then he thought of her . . .*

*An image wobbled before him, glowing and shimmering; he saw Isabella Stevens reaching with her hands into a fire in a square box; blisters were raising on her hands but she kept grabbing at something.*

*His eyes rolled back in his head.*

*He woke. The fragrant grass he stood in reached to his knees. Plump rabbits and fully grown deer darted through a moonlit meadow before him. Shiny fish jumped from a stream.*

*The stars in the skies twirled and danced.*

*Beside him, Great Bear gestured to him and said, "Wusamequin, this is your path. This is the Land Beyond. Your journey begins here."*

*So I have died, he thought.*

*He looked around for his dead wife and child.*

*They have walked on, to the stars, Great Bear said.*

*I shall be alone here, then, Wusamequin replied.*

*His spirit guide shook his head. No. Not alone. Never alone again, Man Split into Two.*

*This is your Way, Wusamequin. Remember it.*

The shaman of the People of the River awoke in his chamber behind the falls. Puffy-eyed but silent, Odina knelt beside his bed, and several Makiawisug sat with her. That gave him pause. The Makiawisug allowed few people to see them. They had never revealed themselves to anyone else in the village except Mahwah. And now, Odina.

What did that mean?

One of them, a little woman, had gathered up the hem of Odina's skirt, as Mahwah's Ti-ti-nay-ah had done, and when she saw that Wusamequin was awake, she shrieked with pleasure.

The Makiawisug began to dance and frolic as they saw that he had come back. They tried to scramble onto him, but Odina shooed them away with her hands.

"Odina," he said.

"Wusamequin." She had been crying. "Do you come back from the Land Beyond to say good-bye?"

"No. I am back," he answered.

They sat in silence. Then she said, "There were pictures on the wall. Of her." She took a deep breath. "You bound yourself to her. She has your spirit."

There was no use in dishonesty. He must leave the earth with a clean heart. "Your words are straight," he admitted. "I put my spirit in a medicine bag, and gave it to her."

"And she took it with her?" Odina queried, her eyes huge with disbelief. When he did not dispute her, she grabbed his shoulders and peered into his face. "And now, because she has left, you're dying! Your spirit is too far from you! Because of her!"

"I'm dying," he confirmed. "Because the bag was destroyed."

"How could you do that?" she shouted at him. "How could you give it to her? Of course she destroyed it! She is a witch! A white skin witch!"

She threw back her head and began to wail a dirge for the dead.

*I cannot believe it was she who destroyed it,* he wanted to tell her.

But it was too difficult to speak. It was too difficult to think.

However, it was very easy to die again.

In her father's quarters, Mahwah lay with her face to the wall. She had lain there for days. They thought she was ill with the pestilence.

*Let them.*

At Colonel Ramsland's order, Mrs. O'Malloy had burned Mahwah's Indian dress and Wusamequin's medicine bag. Without it, she could not see Wusamequin's image. Their bond had been severed.

*I shall never see him again,* she thought.

The shadows lengthened; the sun rose. And set again. She couldn't move, couldn't sleep, couldn't think. She could only grieve.

Her father got better, and came to see her. One late afternoon, he sat beside her bed with a letter in his hands. He reached out and stroked her cheek.

"Poppet, I've wonderful news," he told her. "We're going back to England. There is to be an armed convoy, and we shall go with it." Before she could say anything, he took a breath and added, "And Mrs. DeWitt shall be going with us. As your new mother."

"Oh." She tried to smile, but couldn't manage it. She was shattered. "Dearest Papa, my felicitations."

He reached out and stroked her cheek. "It is my hope that this will bring the color back into your cheeks. The nightmare is ending, my Bella."

"Yes." She swallowed hard. "Yes, Papa." She bit the inside of her cheek to keep from crying.

"Well, then. We shall begin preparations in the morning. We'll be sailing in a fortnight. Not a lot of time to get everything in order."

He patted her shoulder, rose, and left the room.

She sobbed for hours, and then she tried to send out her thoughts, her spirit, her soul.

*My love*, she called. *My love . . .*

But he did not answer her.

Night hung uneasily over the fort. There was talk that the French were advancing. The war would come to Fort William Henry, and soon. Mahwah couldn't help her treacherous thoughts: *Perhaps we shall be prevented from leaving for England.*

*I should almost prefer death, here, than to live in England knowing I should never see him again . . .*

She began to dream of him, seeing his dear face as stars twinkled and danced behind him; she saw him gliding, swooping, circling to a rhythm she could not hear.

*Wusamequin. I miss you.*

Apologizing for bothering her so late at night, Jamie Munsfield came to visit. He wore his uniform jacket all buttoned up, and he looked awkward in it as he sat beside her bed. A child, dressed up in his father's colors.

Licking his lips, he said, "Have you ever been in a battle, Miss Stevens?"

"Just the one," she replied, smoothing her coverlet as she spoke. "With the ... People." When he looked at her uncomprehendingly, she amended, "The Indians."

"I've never been in battle." He swallowed, so young there was only a smattering of beard on his chin. "I ... I'm a bit anxious, I may confess."

She was moved. But before she could say anything—though what words of comfort she could offer, she had no idea—the young man stood.

"I'll be brave, if the time comes," he assured her. Then he straightened his shoulders and raised his chin. "I'm English, after all."

"That you are," she murmured.

He left. She wondered what it would be like to have a son. Wusamequin's son ...

She wept again. Then, exhausted, she fell into a dreamless sleep.

She was shaken awake.

Against flickering candlelight, Odina's face loomed over her. A knife flew against Mahwah's throat and a finger pressed against her lips. Mahwah nodded, silently promising not to cry out.

She sat up and gasped. A candle in a holder beside her bed revealed that Odina was invisible, save for her face, which appeared to float of its own accord in the darkness.

"Have you come to murder me?" Isabella whispered.

The other woman narrowed her eyes with hatred. Isabella gripped the sheets, working out a strategy by which she could save her own life.

*I'll grab the candleholder and smash it over her head. Then—*

Odina whispered, "Wusamequin. *Tah.*" She tapped Mahwah's chest. "*Tah.*"

"Heart?" She grew alarmed. "Wusamequin's heart? Is he all right?"

Odina closed her eyes and allowed her face to grow slack. She looked dead.

"Oh, God, no!" she cried.

In a trice, Odina pushed the knife against her throat, indenting the skin.

"Is he alive? Please, tell me," Mahwah whispered fiercely. "Wusamequin?"

Odina ignored her. She was looking around the room. Then she caught sight of the green-and-brown striped skirt, pale green overblouse, and brown and gold embroidered corset that Mrs. O'Malloy had lent her. Odina crossed to them and plucked them off the pegboard on which they had been hung, tossing them to Mahwah.

"Wusamequin," Odina said.

"You'll take me to him?"

*This may be a trap,* she thought. *Perhaps she thinks to murder me once we're outside the fort. But why would she risk her life to do that?*

She dressed quickly, not caring that Odina watched. Then Odina produced a clay container, which smelled of the lovely flowers the Makiawisug had squeezed to produce the juice of invisibility. Mahwah understood that she had transported it in her invisible clothing.

"I understand," Mahwah said. Taking the container, she dipped her fingers into the liquid. They immediately disappeared. She began to wipe the lotion on her arm.

Then there were heavy footsteps outside the door. Startled, Mahwah jerked.

The clay jar crashed to the floor. The liquid seeped into the wood floor even as Mahwah fell to her knees and tried to soak some of it up in her skirt.

The footfalls paused. "Miss Stevens? Is aught amiss?"

It was Colonel Ramsland.

Odina showed Mahwah the knife. "I'm quite well," Mahwah called back. "I'm so very sorry to disturb you. I dropped something. I—I'll clean it up at once."

"No need to trouble yourself. Mrs. O'Malloy can take care of it the morning."

"All right then. Good night, sir."

"Good night, Miss Stevens."

His noisy boots retreated.

"I'm sorry, I'm so sorry," Mahwah said. Odina

hoisted her to her feet, pushed her in front of herself, and jabbed the tip of the knife between her shoulder blades.

Mahwah sensed that they dare not wait, and yet, it was a risky thing they were undertaking. If only she hadn't dropped the magic potion!

She got to the door, took a breath, and pressed on the latch.

She stepped into the hall, and paused.

There was no one in the corridor.

Then Odina took her hand, leading her. She went in an entirely different direction than Mahwah would have, and navigated twists and turns that finally led to a tiny square cut at the base of a section of fencing. Odina pushed her through, then maneuvered her way through as well. Mahwah thought of the night she and her father had escaped from the hut.

On the other side, Titania, Oberon, Puck, and Cobweb waited. At least a dozen other little people were there as well, huddled together and somber. Mahwah's four raced to her and she picked them up. They clung to her, weeping.

Titania sobbed, "Wusamequin!"

"We'll go to him. We'll go now," Mahwah promised her.

Then she and Odina ran into the dark embrace of the forest.

# ❖ Chapter Eighteen ❖

Tethered in the forest, Odina had brought with her the horses Mahwah's father and Major Whyte had been riding that fateful day. The two women mounted. Mahwah had never ridden astride before, only sidesaddle, and she was amazed at how much easier it was.

They rode all night. In the morning, it rained, washing Odina's protective potion away. The next day it snowed, chilling them both to the bone.

On the third day, they entered the environs of the old village. The cornfields were rotting; the squashes and beans as well.

In the village, the braves worked outside their wigwams, sharpening tomahawks, stringing bows, whittling arrows.

*Are they preparing for war?*

She had no time for further thought, as Odina dragged her into Wusamequin's wigwam.

He was lying on the floor, in his bed. His profile was sharply etched against the shadows. Afraid-of-Everything was curled at his feet; the wolf raised his head and whimpered, forlornly wagging his tail.

"Oh, God," Mahwah murmured as she fell to the ground beside him.

He did not move.

"Wusamequin, it is I, Mahwah," she said brokenly. "Please, don't be dead. I couldn't bear it. Wusamequin . . ."

And then she knew the meaning of the words the Makiawisug had teased them with. She knew what she had always known:

*Nia ktachwahnen* meant that Wusamequin's spirit had called her from England. It had called her to be here, in this moment, with him.

*Nia ktachewahnen* meant that they made magic together, left hand in left hand, soul and spirit together.

*Nia ktachewahnen* meant that together, he and she, they were a new people. Not English, and not of the People of the River. Something that had never existed before.

She took up his limp left hand and placed it over her heart. She pressed her own left hand over his.

"Oh, Wusamequin, you are my love. You are the man of my heart and of my spirit. *Nia ktachwahnen*, my darling," she whispered.

The room burst into a rainbow of light that glistened and gleamed. Drums pounded; she heard the voices of men and women raised in chanting. Very distantly, two wolves howled, raising their voices in chorus.

Stars flashed into existence at the ceiling of the wigwam, then fell toward the earthen floor. Where they touched, flowers sprouted and opened.

Soon the room was a profusion of beauty and light.

And in the center of it, lying on his bed of fragrant grass, Wusamequin opened his eyes. The expression on his face was so much more than a smile; he was glowing; he was overjoyed.

"Mahwah," he said, and her Indian name on his lips was the most wonderful thing she had ever heard.

"Oh, my love, my love," she said in English.

Then he pulled her against himself, tightly. Her heart beat faster; then it grew warm. It seemed to grow inside her body; and then she knew another thing:

She was going to have children with this man.

He held her. He whispered against her neck, "Mahwah. *Nia ktachwahnen.*"

"Wusamequin."

Her heart grew; then she felt warmth and joy blossoming and increasing; when he drew back slightly and looked down at his torso, she saw light emanating from her chest and entering his.

As one, they rose and faced each other, clasping hands.

Then Odina screamed.

"I'm sorry," Mahwah said, turning to her.

But the other woman was not looking at either of them. Her back was to them and she was staring out of the wigwam.

Galloping horse hooves overlaid Wusamequin's shouts as he pushed Mahwah behind himself. He bent down and picked up a tomahawk from beside his bed.

Outside the wigwam, a fife began to play. A drum answered it.

Then a British voice cried, "Fire!" and a musket fired. Another. People began screaming.

Smoke blew into the wigwam.

"We're being attacked!" Mahwah shouted. "It's the British!"

Wusamequin yelled something at her, raced to the doorway, and pulled Odina inside. With a war cry, he jumped over the threshold and raced outside.

Both women flew to the doorway, crowding one another to look out.

Soldiers. Everywhere.

And Colonel Ramsland rode among them.

Odina whirled on Mahwah with death in her eyes.

"They must have followed us!" Mahwah cried. "They must have seen us leave!"

Mahwah pushed past Odina and ran out of the wigwam, realizing too late that she was unarmed. Thick smoke roiled around her, searing her eyes and lungs. She waved her arms in front of herself, attempting to clear her way, but it was no use.

"Wusamequin!" she shouted.

Flintlocks exploded; fires crackled. Orange flames danced in the smoke; red coats blurred all around her. A horse galloped past, grazing her shoulder and throwing her to the ground.

The Yangee soldiers marched through the village in rows like corn. Armed with pistols, war chiefs on horseback shouted orders to them, and they obeyed. They raised their muskets; they fired.

Like harvest rows of corn, People fell.

Oneko had found Wusamequin, and entreated him with gestures to stand with him on a grassy rise above the village.

"You must help us with your medicine," Oneko ordered him. "*Now.*"

Oneko beat a drum to help his shaman find his focus. He was relieved that his medicine man had been restored to vigor, and just in time to help the People. Oneko had seen Mahwah fall in the battle, and he wondered if she had led the Yangees into the village. He knew Wusamequin was worried about her, and that it took every ounce of strength for the medicine man to stay beside him, Oneko, instead of running into the chaos to find her and save her. The young man had already lost one squaw to the Yangees' treachery. It must be terrible on him to face losing another.

For Oneko had accepted the truth of Wusamequin's Way: Mahwah was his new squaw. If they lived through this day, they would make children who stood in both the world of the People and the world of the Yangees.

Sasious was leading the People's defense in the daylight world; Wusamequin had gone to a still place to find help for the People in the veiled world of the spirits.

*From the six directions of the world, I call upon my spirit guide and all his relatives and ancestors,* Wusamequin chanted. *From east, west, north, south, above and below, Great Bear, I call you!*

*I call upon the gods of the winds!*

*I call upon the gods of the clouds!*

*I call upon the gods of fire!*

*The People will die without your assistance!*

The drum pounded. Dying People screamed. Flintlocks erupted.

*It is my right to demand your help!*

He felt the drumming in his blood. He felt his heart grow warm.

A terrible wind rose up, dervishing around Wusamequin and Oneko like thirty demons. It was a storm of wind, whistling and wailing. It gained strength and hurtled itself at the chaos around it. The roofs of wigwams tore away; the rushes and mats ripped free and sailed into the forest. Chestnut trees bent over like old men, straining not to break.

The wind blew the smoke toward the Yangees, who were still marching into the village. Most were on foot; three or four rode horses. Like sky-sized pieces of leather, the smoke hung between them and the People, who were fleeing their wigwams with the children and elders as the braves raced toward the British, most of whom advanced on foot. The smoke acted as a curtain, but it was not substantial. The British flintlocks poked holes in it, and shot at the People.

*It is not enough!*

*Great Bear, I call upon you! I call upon your spirit!*

From his eyes inside himself, Wusamequin knew that the village was aflame. The sweat lodge blazed; Odina's wigwam was half-consumed. His own wigwam was beginning to smoke.

He saw blood in the snow. He saw death in the sky.

Above the shrieking wind, thunder growled. Its depth and volume shook the ground; its intensity quickened Wusamequin's heartbeat.

It was Great Bear, bringing his family.

From the burning forest, the twin of the bear the Yangees had slaughtered a moon before strode forward mightily on his back legs. He roared like an avalanche; he shouted like a waterfall. At his beckoning, more huge black bears burst from the fiery trees and bounded toward the village. They bellowed their rage, most on all fours, some rearing up on their hind legs. Cougars raced into the fracas; deer, moose, and mink darted from the flaming forest to join in the battle against the Yangees.

The bears and animals rushed up behind the Yangees and descended upon the last rank of soldiers. The men began to scream, whirling around to shoot at the animals as teeth and claws flashed and attacked.

But it was still not enough.

There were so many soldiers. So many weapons.

*I demand more help! Where are my relatives? Where are my ancestors? If you do not come, the People will die!*

*Mahwah will die!*

At that thought, his concentration broke; as he

opened his eyes, he saw evil slaughter—braves lying in their own blood, mothers struck down with their children in their arms.

"Mahwah," he whispered, searching with his eyes for her.

He turned to Oneko, and in the same moment, a musket ball slammed into the great sachem's chest. Oneko was thrown backward; blood sprayed from the wound straight up into the sky. Wusamequin dropped to his knees beside him. Oneko's eyes were open but they did not see. His chest was a ruin.

Wusamequin had no medicine to bring the dead back to life again.

The hatred he felt for the Yangees at that moment was unbridled. The fear for Mahwah's life, unquenchable. He felt his heart turn to a tomahawk starved for blood.

He threw back his head and let out a war cry that echoed against the mountains.

Through the musket fire and the screaming, Mahwah heard Wusamequin's voice shouting his rage to the stars themselves. She had been knocked out; now she came to, only to see British soldiers doing unspeakable things. She staggered through the smoke and wind, searching for him. She couldn't believe what she was seeing—the cruelty, the barbarism. She was screaming, "Stop! Stop!" but no one did. No one listened.

*I thought only the French did these things*, she thought,

covering her mouth so that she would not retch. *But it is all of us. We are wrong to be here.*

She cried, "Wusamequin!"

"Mahwah!"

He burst from a wall of smoke and flame. His clothes were half burned off; his leggings shredded around his thighs. The fringes on his jerkin dripped with blood. His hair whipped behind him in the wind.

He grabbed her up in his arms and held her, then swept her up and carried her through hell itself. He dodged musket balls, foot soldiers, and a panicked riderless horse; he avoided braves as they raced to slaughter the enemy.

He carried her to a secluded place slightly above the village grounds. There she saw Oneko, dead, and she fell to her knees and sobbed hard, bitter tears.

The locket containing her parents' miniatures still hung around his neck. She pulled at it; it came free in her hand, and she clasped it under her chin.

Wusamequin took her hand and said, "You must hide, Mahwah. I have strong medicine in me. From you. From Mahwah's strong spirit. I will kill the Yangees. All the Yangees." He touched his chest. "Your *tah* has given me a strong spirit."

As she watched, he closed his eyes and placed both his hands over his heart. Then he drew them slowly away.

A strange energy crackled between his hands. It was like lightning, spitting and exploding in bursts of brilliant white light. Where it hit the ground, flames erupted.

He drew it up above his head and hurled it at six oncoming English foot soldiers.

It exploded in the center of the row, blowing all six to bits.

"No!" she cried. "Oh, no!"

His eyes were glazed, as if he had gone to another place. He put his hands together again. More energy flowed between them. He lifted his hands above his head again—

—and she saw little Jamie Munsfield trudging forward, a musket at his side. His cheeks were smeared with blood.

"Not Jamie! Wusamequin, please, not the boy!" she cried.

He glared at her. "The People die, Mahwah!"

A brave raced up to Jamie and clubbed him over the head. As the boy fell, the Indian scalped him.

Mahwah screamed, "Oh, God, please don't!" she cried. "Oh, Jamie, Jamie!"

But it was too late.

As she wept, Sasious raced toward Wusamequin and her. Though his face was sooty and there was a gash across his cheek, he grinned at Wusamequin. He spoke in their language, pointing at the soldiers. The brave who had scalped Jamie waved his hair in the air.

Mahwah hung onto Wusamequin's left arm, trying to pull his hands apart so that he would make no more death-dealing lightning.

"His death is filled with honor," Wusamequin said.

"No!" she cried. "He was just a boy! It is not filled with honor. They will retaliate! It will never end!"

Then she jumped up and grabbed his left hand.

It was as if a thunderbolt shot through her. He felt it, too, and shouted, "Mahwah!"

Together their clasped hands formed new energy—a shimmering rainbow, surrounded by stars. It undulated and wobbled; then at the far end, perhaps ten feet behind them, Mahwah saw a meadow shimmering in the moonlight. It was ringed with more of the rainbow, which began to sparkle with starlight.

Sasious shouted and raised his tomahawk. He stared at Mahwah and Wusamequin in utter amazement, and began to back away from them.

"What?" she cried, astonished. "What is this?"

"It is the Land Beyond."

"What?"

He cocked his head and raised their joined left hands. The rainbow energy poured from them, surging into the ring that surrounded the twinkling meadow.

Then he spoke to Sasious, who looked horrified, as if he couldn't believe what he was hearing.

"Mahwah," Wusamequin said, his face shining with unearthly light, "The People will go to the Land Beyond. The People will live in the Land Beyond. Safe there. Not hunted there."

He pointed to the braves, women, and children.

One by one, those who were not battling for their lives saw the gleaming magical meadow.

They began to race toward it.

Wusamequin gestured to the ring and began shouting in his language.

Those nearest hurried forward. Then, once they stood within reach of the magical door, they paused.

Wusamequin spoke to them, urging them to go. He kept hold of Mahwah's hand and pointed to the meadow.

To the Land Beyond.

An old man stretched out his hands and spoke rapidly to Wusamequin. Wusamequin nodded at him. The old man turned and faced the People, who were assembling.

Then he tentatively stepped through the rainbow ring. It took but a moment, and then he stood in the meadow, surrounded by light.

He turned and waved, indicating that he was all right. Then he tried to step back through, and could not.

It was a door that opened only one way.

Wusamequin held Mahwah's hand, and called his people to go.

Then Sasious moved into action, planting himself beside the shaman, his tomahawk in his fist.

Wusamequin said to Mahwah, "He says he will stop the People from going to the Land beyond. He says to fight."

"No, Sasious, please," she said, moving toward him.

But Wusamequin yanked her back—just as Sasious's tomahawk swiped the air inches from her face.

Sasious advanced on her. Mahwah screamed; Wusamequin looked from their hands to Sasious, to the doorway, and then back to Mahwah. With his right hand, he yanked the scalping knife from his waist back and hurled it at the war chief. It lodged in his chest.

The People drew back. Sasious gasped, staring down at the wound. He threw his tomahawk at Wusamequin and Mahwah, but it fell far short as he collapsed beside Oneko's corpse.

"What the bloody 'ell?" someone shouted in English.

"Quickly!" Mahwah implored the People. "Go through!"

Wusamequin spoke rapidly, pointing to the soldiers, who had begun marching toward the cluster in front of the doorway. Alerted, a young mother herded her three children toward the doorway. An old woman guided her doddering old man.

But most of the braves would not come. Isabella knew only a few names—Wematin and Ninigret. The burly Tashtassuck, friend of Wusamequin, waved and raced into the smoke, toward the English.

"He says, take People, and go," Wusamequin translated for Mahwah. "He says, Tashtassuck is a warrior and will protect the People."

With the other warriors, Tashtassuck advanced.

A few women—the wives of braves—elected to stay. Many of the old people, as well.

The little boy who had hit Mahwah with a stick tripped across the threshold and ran into the arms of the nearest adult, sobbing for all he was worth.

At Wusamequin's urging, Afraid-of-Everything leaped through, with Mahwah's fairy court riding his back.

Keshkecho ran through.

And then the portal began to lose form. The rainbow, to fade.

The doorway was closing.

The people already in the Land Beyond shouted at Wusamequin and gestured at him, begging him to come, come now! Keshkecho reached out and tried to pull him through, but she could not. Then she began to yell for Odina, who had neither come through, nor could be seen on the battleground.

Wusamequin still held Mahwah's hand. He said to her in English, "We go now."

His dark eyes called to her; his hand enfolded hers. His heart beat inside her own body. But she was English . . . and he was leading his people to a strange, magical place that was their version of the afterlife.

"Isabella Stevens! Come here, girl!" It was Colonel Ramsland himself, advancing on an ebony stallion. She had not seen him with the others. "I know you were forced to leave the fort by that Indian squaw," he continued. "We'll take you back to your father, and all this will be forgotten."

She swallowed hard and took one step toward the colonel.

"Mahwah," Wusamequin said in disbelief.

"My father . . . I'm British," she murmured, shaking all over. "I . . ." She turned to Colonel Ramsland, horribly torn, never dreaming that such a choice would ever be hers to make. "Sir, give me a moment!"

"I am bewildered by your behavior," the man declared. "Have you . . . have you *feelings* for this savage?"

She looked at Wusamequin, then back at the colonel. "Sir, I do."

"I'll make it easier for you then," Colonel Ramsland said. He raised his pistol and aimed it straight at Wusamequin.

"No! No!" Mahwah screamed, spreading her arms wide to shield him.

And in that precise instant, Odina appeared, racing out of the smoke and the carnage. She rammed into Wusamequin as if to knock him through the doorway.

Colonel Ramsland's flintlock discharged, just as Tashtassuck reared up behind him and slammed his leg with his war club. The ball hit Odina in the back, and she crumpled to the ground. Wusamequin bent to pick her up, and in doing so, he let go of Mahwah's hand.

The portal began to vanish.

"Mahwah!" he pleaded, as he stood before it with Odina in his arms. He turned around and handed Odina through. Keshkecho received the wounded woman, lowering Odina gently to the ground.

Wusamequin turned and faced Mahwah, standing outside the portal, while his people shouted his name and urged him to come through.

Behind him, an apparition took form: it was an enormous bear, and it spoke to Wusamequin, who lowered his head.

*Your time has come, Wusamequin.*
*Wusamequin, We of the Land Beyond decree*
*That your time has come.*

*Great Bear, you remind me now that you would show me my path. And that you would help me fulfill the true wishes of my heart.*
*My heart was sick. I wished for it to be healed.*
*My spirit had left me. I wanted it back.*
*These things have been accomplished, for my heart is healed. My spirit is full. I love this English girl, and I will continue to love her whether or not she joins me in the Land Beyond. I cannot speak for her path. I cannot know her truth.*
*But this is my truth: She is my Way, wherever she is.*

Isabella's mind raced. Her heart thundered.
*If Colonel Ramsland's pistol ball had found him . . .*
*. . . if he had died before my eyes . . .*
*I love him. What do I care where we go, how we live? He is my world.*
*My new world.*
*He called me from across the sea. He asked me to come to him. I heard his voice before I knew it was his.*
*He has been calling me, all along.*
*I will answer.*

She turned to Colonel Ramsland, whose horse had reared, thus saving him from a second blow from Tashtassuck's war club.

She called to him, "Tell my father I will always love him!"

As the astonished man looked on, Mahwah leaped into the shining new world with her one true love.

# This is a medicine story. ॐ It tells of a Way.

*The* Way is called "achwahndowagan" in the language of the People.

The Way is called "love" in the language of my father.

The Way is called "Wusamequin" in the language of my spirit.

This Way changed the People. It gave us new hearts. Odina is my sister now. Keshkecho, as well. Wabun-Anung is my *nomasis*, my little grandmother.

During Harvest Moon, the Makiawisug made blankets for my first-born son, Phillip Wauntheet Monnitoow. Phillip Shining Spirit. Titania is his godmother.

A year and a half later, during Strawberry Moon, they made blankets for my daughter, Emily Mahkwa, which means Bear, in honor of her father's spirit guide.

We live in the Land Beyond. Someday we will walk the Road of Stars. For now, we walk together, our family and our tribe. We call ourselves the Spirit People.

Let those who hear my story grow strong in their own spirits. Let those who hear my story grow strong in *achwahndowagan*.

> Let them become Warriors of the Heart, as my people and I have become.
> Let them find True Love, as I have found.
> That is my Way.

—Mahwah Stevens, Wife of Wusamequin, in the Land Beyond

# Author's Note

This retelling of *Beauty and the Beast* is set during the French and Indian War, which lasted from 1756–1763. Fort William Henry was an actual British fort, but it was commanded in 1756 by Lt. Colonel George Monro. However, Lt. Colonel Monro never followed Mahwah back to Wusamequin's village, nor massacred any of his people. Therefore, I have invented the character of Colonel Ramsland for the purposes of my story. Mohican, Delaware, Mohegan, and other neighboring tribes traditionally are grouped as "Algonquin" Native American tribes, and I have used a mixture of names from that cluster for my Native American characters. For this reason, I have referred to Wusamequin's tribe as "the People of the River," and not as "the people who live alongside a river which ebbs and flows," which is a more traditional way to refer to the Mohican people. However, the majority of names are Mohican, and the language they speak in *Spirited* is Mohican. The Makiawisug are the little people of the Mohegans.

I have also put my own twist on the beliefs of the Algonquins in the afterlife. Many tribes and clans had their own interpretations of the Land Beyond, although the Milky Way was referred to by many as the Road of Stars, walked by spirits and ancestors on their celestial journey.

My inspirations for this retelling were twofold: First, James Fenimore Cooper's novel, *The Last of the Mohicans: A Narrative of 1757*, which was originally published in 1826. The second was the 1992 film by the same title, starring Daniel Day-Lewis and Madeleine Stowe. However, in both cases, the title is a misnomer: the Mohican Nation is alive and well, with over fifteen hundred enrolled members, over half of whom live on the Stockbridge-Munsee Reservation in Wisconsin.

*Nancy Holder* has published approximately sixty books and over two hundred short stories, essays, and articles. Her work has been translated into over two dozen languages, and has appeared on recommended lists in the *Los Angeles Times*, on amazon.com, and other bestseller lists. It has also appeared on recommended reading lists of the American Library Association, the American Reading Association, the New York Public Library Books for the Teen Age, and others. She has received four Bram Stoker Awards for her supernatural fiction. She has written many titles for Simon & Schuster, including dozens set in the *Buffy the Vampire Slayer* and *Angel* universes. With Debbie Viguié, she cowrote the *Wicked* saga, about two feuding witch families in Seattle. She is also the author of *Pearl Harbor: 1941*. She lives in San Diego with her eight-year-old daughter, Belle, who is currently franchising lemonade stands in their neighborhood in order to raise money for innumerable animal causes. Contact Nancy at www.nancyholder.com. The Holder women are owned by their cats, David and Kittnen Snow, and their dog, Dot.

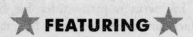

**Season Howe is a witch on the run for a horrible crime that happened** three centuries ago—a crime so awful, her punishment will last forever.

Daniel Blessing is the handsome stranger who has spent a lifetime hunting the evil witch.

Kerry Profitt, an innocent college student, doesn't believe in witches at all.

But Daniel's quest is about to bring Kerry and Season together in the strangest of ways—a way that will make Kerry believe all too well. . . .

**Summer. Fall.
Winter. Spring.**

**Four seasons,
one incredible
adventure.**

Witch Season: Summer
Available July 2004 from Simon Pulse

# ❀ WANTED ❀

## Single Teen Reader in search of a FUN romantic comedy read!

*How Not to Spend Your Senior Year*
BY CAMERON DOKEY

*Royally Jacked*
BY NIKI BURNHAM

*Ripped at the Seams*
BY NANCY KRULIK

*Cupidity*
BY CAROLINE GOODE
(COMING SOON)

*Spin Control*
BY NIKI BURNHAM
(COMING SOON)

★ *Available from Simon Pulse* ★

✱ *Published by Simon & Schuster* ✱